Run of the Arrow

BY

Michael Rutter

Copyright © 2003 Michael Rutter
All Rights Reserved

This is a work of fiction. All characters are fictional and any resemblance to persons living or dead is purely coincidental.

No part of this book may be reproduced in any form whatsoever, whether by graphic, visual, electronic, filming, microfilming, tape recording, or any other means, without the written permission of the author, except in the case of brief passages embodied in critical reviews and articles where the title, author and ISBN accompany such review or article.

Published and Distributed by:

Granite Publishing and Distribution, LLC
868 North 1430 West
Orem, Utah 84057
(801) 229-9023 • Toll Free (800) 574-5779
Fax (801) 229-1924

Page Layout & Design by Myrna Varga • The Office Connection, Inc.
Cover Design by Steve Gray

ISBN: 1-932280-06-5
Library of Congress Control Number: 2003101166
Printed in the United States of America

First Printing, August 2003

10 9 8 7 6 5 4 3 2 1

Acknowledgments

To my late father, Paul, who helped me catch my first fish and taught me how to shoot—whose stories and love of the old West brought the past to life.

To my son Jon-Michael, my outdoor partner, friend, and editor.

To Kasey, Gary, and Kirby, my outdoor friends, mountain men at heart lost in the 21st century.

Chapter 1

The brave rode calmly out of the afternoon sun. He must have cut loose from the others, bringing up their back trail like he was. The lone warrior knew I'd seen him, but he kept on coming, walking his spotted stallion toward me.

I figured I was in big trouble since it's serious business facing a mounted warrior when you're a foot. Then, without fanfare, he dug his heels into that pony's sides and came at me on a dead run. He lowered his war lance and shifted his shield. I dropped my bow, struggling for the rifle strapped on my shoulder. With clumsy fingers, I fought to get it free just in time.

In a flash he was on me.

Sidestepping his pony at the last second, getting out of the way of those killer hooves, I brought my rifle up like a staff to check his lance. The wooden shaft below the point fractured on my barrel. I could feel the owl feathers brush past my face. I spun back so sharply, I dropped my Hawken while his spotted mount turned like a buffalo pony and came for me again.

The tall brave wheeled his broken lance at me as I twisted sideways toward him, fighting to grab it. Splinters bit into my left hand as I got a solid hold with my right. Good thing for me he had his wrist strap on. With all my strength I leaned back putting my weight into the effort. He slid off his horse with a thud but was up and facing me in a wink, his shield guarding his chest, swinging his lance with the other hand. I stepped back, missing a powerful blow that would have busted my head open wide like a split tomato. I rushed in, which surprised him, and jerked him over my shoulder and up in the air.

I could have shot him with my cap and ball pistol, but I didn't want to attract the others if I could help it. He lost some wind when he hit the ground, giving me time to draw my knife. I lunged for his chest, but my blade deflected off his shield and he sent me backwards with a foot in my ribs. Discarding that shield, he plunged at me with the chisel pointed back-end of his broken lance. He savagely jabbed for my stomach, but by good fortune I dodged his blows. He got careless after a dozen pokes. With a desperate effort to stab me some more, he came in too close and I laid open his arm with the razor-tip of my knife. He dropped the shaft and stepped back, grabbing his arm.

He bolted toward his broken spear point—which was still a formidable weapon. He picked it up and smiled at me. That spear point was long enough to be a knife blade. The afternoon sun reflected in the sweat on his copper face. He rushed me but I snatched up the shaft and buried the chisel-point end of the war lance in his calf and hit him a good one on the side of his head, knocking him out. He was going to have a sore leg for a week or two and a big headache tomorrow. I gathered my bow and weapons and got out of the meadow like a scalded polecat. The first thing to do was to get myself out of this wide-open park and get into the safety of the thick timber. This was a close call and I knew it.

Well, I guess I better introduce myself. You probably don't know me, least not yet. Most folks know my famous cousin, Orin Porter Rockwell, who bodyguarded the Mormon prophets. He was arrested once with Joseph Smith and protected him a number of times—Brigham Young, too. Anyway, my name is Wolf Rockwell and right now I'm all alone. Well, all alone except for some Crow braves who want to scalp me. And that's alone in a bad way. Unless I miss my guess, they'll not only want to part my hair, they'll want my possibles and furs, especially after I've wounded one of their own.

I've been trapping furs for the Mormon people who settled the Great Basin country. They need warm winter clothes and the area where they've been homesteading has long been trapped out. Besides, they're mostly a bunch of plowing farmers. Brother Brigham, as they call him, would rather have his Mormon men busting sod, leaving the trapping to folks like me. There's no market for beaver anymore, so it's pretty lucky when a mountain man can sell anything with fur he can catch. They pay good cash money, too. It's been a good season's catch and I'm loaded down.

But so much for trapping.

I am feeling a little scared. You can bet your farm those Crow braves know I'm here. They're not sure quite where I'm at, but they know I'm about some place. They've likely helped themselves to my four horses and they don't plan to return them. They've also got my truck. I hate losing my second Hawken rifle. She's a bit worn but you can bet that gun shoots plenty straight. There wasn't much food left after trapping all winter—some coffee, packs of elk jerky, and a few pounds of beans. But there's the rest of my possibles, a beat up coffee pot I won from a Canadian trapper after a foot race, what's left of my extra lead and powder, my winter clothes, some Hudson wool blankets, my best axe, twelve Miles Standish traps . . . and all my winter's trappings which are a considerable fortune, at least to me.

Whether they're waiting for me or moving on, I don't know. With Crow you never know. Without my coat I'd be getting chilly as soon as that spring sun dropped behind the peaks the Indians call Wind Rivers. It's a lonely country, but lovely. It's a place where the trails blend into the forests and clearings and valleys—all of which kind of fade into the next set of mountains. Well, as best I can tell, there are six of them and one of me. I suppose a man in this country can't walk too lightly. I can tell you one thing, though, if them folk take off with my horse, rifle, and gear, I'm going to get it back. That's just the way I am.

Now stealing is second nature to Indians, especially Crows. They don't think like we do. Even if they don't need what you've got, they'll steal it for sport and they'll think you're a better man if you can steal it back without their knowing. If there's no good reason for fighting and stealing, they'll make one up and go at it. To them, it's just a big game—a deadly game, but a game these men were bred to play. They're not called braves for acting like cowards. Doing daring things is how you prove you are a man in this world.

About now, I'm feeling like a beaver with the tip of his tail caught in a trap. It's been this way for a thousand years, I suppose, or for however long they've been here. And it isn't likely they'll stop just because we might try and civilize them. Indians love to fight and Crows seem to love it most. Well, maybe they like stealing horses more. I'm not sure. They're a proud people and I respect them.

I've been living in Crow territory for some time now, so I knew their ways. Like I was saying, they don't look at stealing your truck the same way a white man does. They don't have the same concept of ownership we have, either. I heard of some missionaries who went to live with the Indians on the Great Plains. They tried to teach the Sioux about the white man's god and about the Ten Commandments. To make a long story short, one of those Bible-thumping missionaries with a snoot full of arrogance was giving a hell fire message about stealing when an old brave had heard enough. He got up and lifted this preacher's hair as neatly as you speak.

A good thief is a revered man in the tribe, a man who has as much status as a banker would in a city. I've never had much use for bankers but I understand Indians. I surely don't hate them, not at all. It's simply in their upbringing up to steal, just as it's in a mountain lion's nature to stalk. Still, I was just mad enough to be reckless about doing something to get my gear back. I knew they'd found my camp by now. They didn't have me yet, though, and I understood this game, too. I like to think I understood it as well as any mountain man . . . or as well as any Crow.

It was only a stroke of luck that I stopped to make my camp when I did. It was a few hours back. They might have caught me pants down, unsuspecting, otherwise. My hair could have been hanging from the lance of some brave. I was coming out of the high country with my pelts, keeping an eye peeled for trouble, but maybe I enjoyed the day too much. Maybe I wasn't paying as much attention to my back trail as I should have. Anyway, I decided to stop and make early camp. I was heading to the Green River to meet with some friends and rest up. Then I was going to cross over to the Salt Lake Basin and sell my furs to Brigham Young and visit some of my Mormon kinfolk thereabouts. Maybe I'd even spark a few gals with my cousin Kip. He has more wives than I have horses.

I made my camp early in the afternoon, like I said. It was a well-concealed camp to any casual observer, but there's no way I could mask my trail completely. If an Indian cuts your back tracks, and they're fresh, you're always in for trouble. I needed to take some time and do some hunting. I was almost out of meat and craved roast since most of my supplies were used up. I'd been moving steady for several days leaving little sign, so I thought an early camp would be safe. Besides, I was almost out of their territory.

I'd seen a deer trail a canyon back, so I thought I might work my way along the ledge and see if I could scare myself up some fresh venison. After picketing my horses and gathering wood for the evening fire, I took up my rifle and my bow. I usually hunted with my bow so I could save lead and an arrow is quiet. I always liked to ramble about and explore new country. Wandering and solitude has been my life. My older cousin Orin always teased me about liking to be by myself too much. I never was as sociable as he was, even if he's seven different kinds of poison when mad. A man would do well not to push him. Otherwise, he's a friendly sort and folks just seem to cotton toward him. Back home at dances and such, the girls would just sort of blush when he asked them. I'd usually hang around back, listen to the fiddle music and maybe get into a nice friendly fight. All the time I'd rather be out hunting coons with the hounds. But not cousin Orin. He'd dance the shoes off all them Mormon gals. It was always a curious thing to me how he could have all those women hanging off him. Everyone knew he was as mean as the devil. Even heard some people thought he was the devil himself.

I've always felt more at home toting a good rifle and exploring the woods than being sociable. I've never had a silver tongue, but I'm told I've got mighty hard fists and I know I shoot pretty straight. I was certain to need all my skills before the day was over. Don't get me wrong, I wasn't looking for trouble, far from it. But if trouble took me, I'd come back at her head on . . . with my rifle cocked and my hands fisted.

They say a man who lives in wild country shouldn't daydream much—a good way to end up cold and fitted with wings. I was just darned lucky I didn't stumble right into that band. I was just putting a final stalk on a small mule buck, crossing a meadow and enjoying the warm afternoon, looking forward to spring after a long winter. Then I saw unshod tracks that were fresh. Too fresh!

The tracks had been made in the last five minutes. Moisture was still forming along the sides in the mud. And they were heading in the general direction of my camp. They'd been following my sign directly. If I hadn't gone hunting, they might have taken me. I could see it plain by the sign. A man doesn't have to be an expert woodsman to know. The tracks told the story. These braves were hunting me. It was when I looked up from the sign that I saw the brave on the horse who came at me.

You won't keep much hair in these mountains if you're careless. As you'd expect, I got out of that meadow fast, re-priming the load in my rifle as I went. The brave's horse had run back the direction he'd come. I took stock of my gear. I always tried to keep my horn packed and an ample supply of lead on my person. I loosened the smooth bore .52 caliber pistol shoved into my belt, so I could get at it fast. It used the same ball as my rifles—wasn't much good at a distance, but up close it could open up a man. I had my bow and a half-dozen arrows. Like any mountain man I also carried a knife. Mine was built by a fellow named James Black down Arkansas way. They tell me he was the same fellow who made Jim Bowie's famous knife. My Arkansas toothpick, like that Bowie knife, had a clipped point and the same kind of cross guards. The only difference was it weighed less and was a little easier to stone. It was mighty sharp. Once I tried shaving with it. I cut up my face real bad but it kind of worked. You can get a knife shaving sharp, but it's not much good for whiskers. In the mountains, a knife is a man's best friend. When your powder's wet or you're out of lead, it's always ready. It's an iron mistress. As you can tell, I'm a man who appreciates good weapons. Out here, they're tools a man's life depends on.

    I don't care much about clothes, as long as they're warm and last a good while. Give me buckskins or a spun shirt over fancy shirts and britches. I once wore a store-bought suit, though, back in Missouri when I was visiting with Orin and kin. Yes sir, I had to borrow it and I'm not ashamed to admit it. My auntie insisted I wear that store-bought suit while I watched her relations get baptized by Mr. Joseph Smith himself, the Mormon Prophet. I called him Brother Joseph. He was a fine man and I can say that since I knew him—even had dinner at his house once. He asked me if I wanted to be baptized. Of course, I said no since I wanted to remain a God-fearing heathen. He was a Christian man who would do anything to help, even if it was his last dollar. I was personally sad when I found out that pond-scum mob killed him. Anyway, the baptism took place in a muddy river near the farm. Auntie said I looked real gentleman-like standing there. I felt like a broke-down plow mule with a fancy $75 saddle strapped on his back. I'd have traded my duds for a rusty trap or a pound of moldy jerky. Couldn't wait to get back into something useful.

A while after my visit, I was back home in Ohio. I was up early to milk our cows. As far as I can tell, someone in my house knocked over a coal-oil lamp. My family died in that fire. I buried my father and brother with my own hands near the orchard trees on the hill. I never did find the bodies of my mother or my sisters. I went down to a town called Nauvoo on the Mississippi where my kin had moved and stayed with them for a time. The Mormons are good people and I respect them. I did what I could to help out. But I didn't take much to the rigors of religion even if I did mostly believe. It's all right for other folks if that's what they want. It's just not for me. As I said, I'm a God-fearing heathen who wanted to be a mountain man. Besides, all that praying, preaching, and rules keeping—and farm work— didn't set well with a man bound to go West and see the mountains. Things were kind of hard. I took off to be a mountain man because I wasn't cut out to be a farmer or a Mormon. The beaver trade had pretty much died, but I wanted to see the shining mountains they called the Rockies.

I got my wish. I was in the Rockies all right—maybe about to lose my life—but I was a mountain man and proud of it, by Jove. I'd not want to be anywhere else! With all the care I could muster, I worked my way back to my camping place as the sun was getting low in the western sky.

Chapter 2

The edges of the clouds in the afternoon sky were charged with flowing streaks of scarlet-crimson. Mountain men refer to it as Wind River cloud fire. It glowed against the dark peaks like a dying campfire. It was an empty, lonesome land. You had to tread light if you wanted to keep your hair, step carefully and keep your eyes open.

Had the Crows looted my camp by now?

Best not go barging in since it might be a trap. When I'd gone hunting, I let my hobbled horses feed on the early-spring grass. There was a creek a hundred yards down the gentle slope and a rocky canyon at my back. It was protected from the wind and barely visible from a casual glance. It would work against me. Other than the usual precautions, I wasn't covering my trail. Mind you, I wasn't leaving more sign than I had to. My plan had been to move fast and quick. Crows could find a trail when there wasn't one. Left

Foot Bill, the man who taught me how to trap when I first came to the mountains as a boy, used to say, "Them damned Crows can follow a Tennessee cricket across slick rock—even tell when that ol' cricket stopped to eat. They ain't human, they ain't. Once on the Yallowerstone, a pack of Crows followed me across barely nothing. Took luck to get off with my life—lost my furs and horses."

Only a greenhorn takes the same trail twice in this country. It makes it too easy for an enemy to lay in wait. Left Foot was right. A human is a creature of habit and if he's not careful he gets too comfortable. Even if I hadn't seen those tracks, I'd have made my way back to camp by a different route and done it carefully. I had on moose-hide moccasins. I was glad of it since I could feel even the smallest twigs with my toes. I always wore moccasins when I was hunting or trapping. I wore boots for riding and working around stock.

I carefully worked my way back until I could overlook my camp from a ridge. Long shafts of light fingered eagerly between the clefts of a rocky crag, then started to fade reluctantly as the sun dropped over the horizon. The creek that ran beyond my camp lost its green color and turned chocolate brown. High in the dull sky, a hawk screamed out, floated in large circles, then disappeared with the light. I sure would like to have been that hawk. I checked my load again, though I didn't need to. A gun not ready to shoot is just a club. I always kept my weapons loaded and treated them accordingly. Too many folks are shot with unloaded guns. With mine, there's no doubt. They're loaded for bear. I tied my bow on my back but I kept her strung.

I was a coyote after a snowshoe hare. I came closer. The hair on the back of my neck was standing up, and I was sure I could smell Indian. I knew if I got upwind, a brave could smell me. I hadn't backed into a bar of soap all winter. Like a nervous gray squirrel, I peeped about the side of a smooth rock. I could see my camp below in the waning light. I couldn't see where they were exactly, but I could feel them. They were waiting someplace, waiting the way wolves wait near a water hole. Every move I made gave them an advantage.

I had to out think them. They had me outnumbered, but I was dealt cards in this game and I was going to play them. Indians, especially Crows, were hard to guess and that was my biggest problem. What were they going to do? Were they in a hurry and eager to move on so I could hold tight? Would they move on and then come back to hunt me later? Were they waiting, hoping I'd come back to camp as if nothing was up? Had they found the other brave?

As I peered over the top of the ridge, I could see my horses where I'd left them. The warriors were counting on me not knowing they were there. They planned a surprise . . . they'd lift my scalp as well as take my horses and gear. If I did this right, the surprise could be turned on them. I'd slip down and sneak off with my horses and truck and maybe a few of their horses, too, for my time. They owed me that much. I'd stolen more than one horse. For that matter, I'd stolen many a watermelon and never got whooped for it.

As I inched closer, I kept an eye on my stock. Nothing had been touched. I was about to creep closer when I saw a slight movement in the pine brush a hundred yards down. There he was, sitting in the bush, waiting to jump me if I came down that draw, as any man naturally would coming back to his camp not expecting trouble. Walking down a handy gully is a lot easier than breaking a trail through the thick spruce choked with dead falls, especially if that man's been off hunting and has meat down.

He was cagey, that Indian. He'd picked a good place to hide. It's where I'd have been. I studied the situation, looking over the slope and gully for at least five minutes, trying to decide if there be other braves close about. After watching him, I noticed he paid careful attention to the draw, seeming to ignore the slope directly above—an unlikely place for a body to walk down. There was a thick carpet of grass and a few big rocks. Otherwise it was a gentle slope. The light was nearly gone, but a full moon was creeping up on the horizon, giving shape to the surrounding landscape.

I couldn't take them all at once, but I could fight them one at a time. I made mental notes about the land, looking at it harder than a man would who wasn't afraid. As careful as a weasel raiding a chicken coop, I worked my way down the edge of spruce so I could get behind him. He was very still, just like one of those Greek statues I'd seen in a book. If he hadn't moved earlier, I might have walked into his trap. Now with luck, maybe I'd turn the tables. It took me twenty minutes to work my way above him. The rocks and aspens had taken on a glowing white, ghost-like color. I'm quiet on the stalk, but I was encouraged by a light breeze that helped cover my sound. I lost sight of him as I crept closer. I kept wondering if he might have heard me and was waiting someplace else. I fought down the impulse to melt into that thick stand of timber and let them try to find me.

I could just see the silhouette of his head by the pine boughs. He hadn't moved. I could also see the knife in his right hand and the iron head of the hawk in the other. I put a thick aspen between us and closed in. I was ten feet away when I felt a gut-load of panic. It took a good five minutes, but it seemed like five hours getting into springing range. At anytime, if he turned, he'd see me. I knew

I could take him, but I had to do it quietly so I'd not alert the others. The breeze was in my face. He smelt of sweat, rancid bear grease, and buffalo guts.

I needed another yard. I inched up my left foot, but I dislodged a twig ever so slightly. If I hadn't have felt it, I'd never have heard it. But not that brave. With a slightly startled jerk, he turned his head about and knew the hunter had become the hunted. As quick as a rattlesnake, he swung his hawk back. I could also see the gleam of the blade in the moonlight—his knife poised for a strike.

He was agile, too, like a mountain cat twisting and lunging uphill at me. Instead of claws, his paws clutched tomahawk and knife. I reacted without a thought, swinging back, driving the barrel end of my rifle at him. I missed his arm, but it was just as well. That Hawken didn't do his smile any good. Unlike my cousin Orin, I avoided killing this man. Yes, I knew both braves I'd fought would gladly have laid me out if given a chance, but this was my way. I did, however, help myself to his weapons. I checked his rifle and found it was loaded and ready to go. He wasn't going to need it for a time. I hid his knife and hawk under some brush and went on. Two down . . . five to go. I thought.

If I could, I'd take all their horses. Walking home would teach them to trouble Wolf Rockwell. Indian horses weren't the best, but they'd bring a few dollars at Bridger and stealing them would please me. I was starting to get a bad feeling, a feeling I couldn't shake. My good sense told me I ought to cut my losses and disappear, but it just wasn't the Rockwell way. The wind had stopped. The evening air should have been cool and refreshing, but it felt heavy and stifling.

Something didn't feel right. The sounds of the night, sounds that tell you nothing is lurking about, were absent. I untied the thong on my knife and tried to calm the tightening in my chest. Could they hear my heart pounding? I had to keep going or I'd lose my nerve. I dearly wanted a warm fire, a strong cup of coffee, and a piece of rare meat. I was a fool walking about in the dark like this. I couldn't do much until daylight now anyway and I knew it. I could stumble into another trap. I would scout a little more then I'd best be finding a place to hide in the rocky cliffs.

I never saw him coming.

The only thing that saved my life was that I shifted my rifles. A Hawken shooter isn't a goose-down pillow and I had two to carry. I thought I'd relieve my arms and rest the rifle butts on the ground while I studied the layout.

Shifting the guns and squatting down threw his timing off. He leaped over a rotting log, knife in hand, and hit both rifle barrels squarely, flipping them out of reach. If he was stunned, he didn't show it. Nor did he let go of his knife, a trading butcher, the type sold to Indians by Ramsay Crooks or William Ashley. The blades were made of soft steel but were easy to sharpen. They were just right for lifting a man's scalp, cleaning a buffalo, or gutting a guy like me.

It happened so fast all I saw was a moving gleam in the moonlight. I'd fallen backwards, quickly reaching for my own knife. He lunged and I parried. I thrust and nicked the side of his stomach. I was less accustomed to knife fighting than he, but I was stronger and bigger. That made us about equally matched for a fight to the death. I wondered if my bones would bleach in the sun? My father had died before he could realize his dreams. Would the same fate befall me? Would I see eighteen? The brave came at me again. I reacted. I'd only practiced at knife fighting, not done it for real. Left Foot Bill said I was pretty good for a pilgrim who'd never fought when it really mattered, but there was no replacing experience. On the banks of the Green, we'd spent many hours practicing with carved-wood knives. I was glad I'd paid attention. At least I knew how to anticipate my opponents' next moves and a few ways to block them. It's surprising how much better you can see in moonlight when you know you might get stabbed.

I was keeping up when I saw my chance. I made a quick side step and trapped his knife arm next to my body. Now he was more on my terms. I grabbed his arm, my knife still in my hand, flipping him over my shoulder as I'd often done wrestling with the men in camp. The warrior had thought he had me with that last lunge. When his blade missed my middle, he was off balance. He landed on his back with all the breath out of him. With my left hand I quickly shifted my knife to my mouth, holding it in my teeth. Still holding his wrist with my right, I jerked him swiftly up and kicked him for all I was worth. Then I did it again. I twisted his arm and flipped the dazed brave again. I ripped his arm upward, wrecking his shoulder. I was less likely to be followed if there were wounded who had to be cared for. I didn't take killing a man lightly if there was another way around it. I made a mental note to learn more about knife fighting since I'd gotten lucky.

I got up to look for my rifles just in time to see the butt of my own Hawken flashing toward my skull.

CHAPTER 3

I might have been in worse scrapes, but I don't know when.

When I awoke, I was powerful thirsty. My head pounded so hard I could scarcely think straight. The stars started spinning when I lifted my head. The dying campfire gave off little warmth. Waves of nausea swept across me. I was as dizzy as a man with Nauvoo fever. Something trickled past my eye and mouth. It was warm and salty. It was blood. My blood!

I fought through the haze, trying to make sense of what had happened. I remembered catching my breath after the knife fight, then the butt end of a rifle and the lights went out. That was all I remembered. I was hurting too bad to be scalped, so I knew they hadn't killed me yet, even though I felt like it.

How long they'd watched the fighting, I don't know. I was occupied, keeping that brave from knifing me open. Indians, especially Crows, are funny about this sort of thing. They have a code and they live up to it. They'll sneak in, kill you, or steal our stock, but they live by their own idea of fair play and fighting. Respecting bravery and combat skills, it wasn't their way to jump in, even if one of their own was getting his ears pinned. They'd wait for the outcome, then they'd kill you or save you for some future torture. Personal courage was measured by how your enemy fought. It was big medicine to bring back a brave captive. To Crows, an enemy's courage was also measured by how much torture he could take. If they thought you brave, you died with their respect. You were still dead, mind you, but respected. I guess if you had to go, it's a whole lot better to go out clean. Once they start on you, you're pretty much dead anyway. Me, I was always determined to die like a man, but I wanted to postpone it for as long as I could. Was I was being saved for another day? My head hurt too much for me to worry about it now.

The left side of my forehead felt caved in. I reckoned the gash must have opened again and was bleeding. My head felt hot, but the rest of me was cold. There was a tattered blanket over me unlike the warm wool blankets the braves had. I was lying on the bare ground which was downright cold this time of the year. I wasn't sure if my muscles ached from the cold or from the fight. Two leather ropes were looped around my neck and tied to the wrists of braves sleeping on either side of me. If I tried to move or escape, they'd feel it instantly and be awake. Thick leather thongs secured my wrists and elbows together. They'd used my rope to lash my feet. I remember thinking that if my head didn't hurt so bad, the way I was tied would be painful enough.

I needed a drink, but it took all my energy to turn a little and rise up on my elbows. One of the braves started to stir, but it didn't matter. I must have passed out. Just as well since I wouldn't have been fit company. Unconscious, I wouldn't keep thinking about how much I needed to get to that creek.

Dawn greeted me with a savage kick in the ribs, making me gulp. I looked into the face of a tall brave with a wide, white scar across his cheek and lip. Besides that battle scar, the most noticeable thing about him was his hair. It was a greasy jet-black and thick, flowing out, touching his shoulders and back like a lion's mane. His bangs were several inches long and waxed with bear grease straight up in a pompadour, making him look tall and predatory like a hawk.

His dirty-chestnut leggings of tanned elk hide were stained with blood. A faded yellow loincloth clad his middle. It was held in place by a buckskin strap. The knife at his side was handy. A bearskin vest touched his waistband, and he had on my powder horn and possibles bag. My heavy jacket was draped over his shoulders. Crows always had the good sense to cover up when it was cold. Some of the tribes, like the Canadian Crees, went bare chested even in the dead of winter.

Crows were the best dressed and, in my opinion, the most vain of all the tribes I'd met. Scar, as I called him, was a dandy. Even on the warpath, he fussed with his hair like a giddy schoolgirl. He put a dab of grease on his bangs every morning to make them stand up, combing the rest with a buffalo tongue. I thought fondly about removing some of his fancy hair with a dull scalping knife. He had cruel lips, squinty eyes, and grunted something when he noticed I was watching him. He drew back to kick me. I tried to grab his leg but my reflexes were a bit sluggish with my head still spinning.

I felt his savage moccasin in my ribs. But I'd seen it coming, so I was able to move back a little. I could see he had my second rifle. I hoped he would over-charge it and blow off part of his pretty face. In a motion faster than I thought possible, he unsheathed his knife and swung it about my nose. At least it would end fast. He brought the polished blade down, slicing the thongs on my hands, taking a little of my skin with it. I felt fresh blood rush to my stiff fingers. Pulled by the leather neck rope, I was dragged toward the stream. He kindly shoved my face down into the icy pool, cutting my legs free as I panicked for air. After the first shock of the water, I drank deeply and bathed the welt on my head. I drank again and dunked my head in the ice-cold stream. Surges of life and shivers of cold ran through my body, but it felt good. What I wouldn't give now for a large cup of coffee.

I looked at the spruce on the west slope of the hillside. The trees were a blue-green. Under different circumstances I'd have stared at them for a while. The aspen were starting to get leaves and the grass by the stream was already a thick emerald green. This would be a good place to build a cabin for a man who loved a view. I wondered if I'd ever get back here. For that matter, I wondered if I'd see another sunset.

A harsh tug on the rope pulled me out of the water and onto the frosty bank. Scar threw me a large piece of jerky and pointed toward the horses. It was moose jerky and tasted good. It ought to since I'd smoked it. They'd helped themselves to my truck, that was plain to see. I sucked the meat slowly, getting it soft before I chewed it, not knowing when I'd eat again. Indians were usually liberal about feeding a captive the same food they ate. If there was a lot of food, you ate as well as they did. If there was little to eat, you starved along with them. At least I knew we'd eat well until my food ran out.

They threw my saddle on one of my packhorses. That saddle cost me a month's trapping and I was glad they brought it. Scar and another brave who happened to be wearing my hat lifted me bare back on my horse, Blue. He's ugly and doesn't look like much of an animal, which is probably why they put me on him, but he's a mountain-bred mustang that's long-legged and all heart. Scar never let go of that rope about my neck.

A brave wearing buffalo horns held the rope to Blue. He never said much, but he watched everything that was going on. Another brave who looked wet behind the ears stood looking about. He carried a coup stick to touch an enemy in battle. He was out to make a name and establish himself as a brave. He had a bow and arrows on his back in an antelope quiver in case counting coup got old and he wanted to stick someone. He eyed my rifles fondly, the one on the pack pony and the one Scar claimed as his own.

He draped an elk cape about his shoulders. In the evenings he wore leggings made from a Hudson Bay blanket, which many Crows seemed to favor.

I wanted to give old Blue the hardest kick of his life and then let them try and find me once I got across that meadow. In my mind I saw myself riding away. Had I not been roped, I might have made a play, taking my chances on yanking my horse's lead from Buffalo Horns. It's hard to hit a man at a dead gallop. I'd have taken my chances on that, too. But, when they've got you and your horse snugged up, all you can do is wish.

When I was seated, Scar backhanded me across the mouth and sent my head spinning again. I took it without a whimper. Crows like to see how much a man can take. It's their way to honor a captive—dishing out punishment. I figured if I had to die, I might as well go out showing them I was brave. But if I got a chance, old Scar would be the first dance ticket I'd punch.

My horse is a good mount, like I said. He's mountain-bred but he isn't noted for having a smooth gait. Normally it doesn't bother me. However, when a man's without his saddle and has had his head all busted, every bump can be a nightmare. I vowed not to cry out or show fear. Yet, with every step my horse took, I wasn't sure if I was going to lose my stomach or if my head would just bounce off down the canyon. I was queasy as a greenhorn hung over from his first rendezvous. Several times I felt myself slipping, and I grabbed onto the mane for my life, anything to keep from sliding off. Scar would have thought it quite a trick to snap my neck otherwise. By mid morning, I was starting to get used to the pace. That or my head was so numb I didn't care.

I took some comfort in knowing that I was at least as well off as the braves I'd fought. A couple braves were in serious pain—another was rolled up in a blanket. He must have died. There was an anguished look in the eyes on one man and a permanent grimace on the other fellow's mouth, especially when the trail got rough. I couldn't feel too sorry for myself.

I took a certain amount of pride knowing I'd held my own, that I'd taken three out of action. Remember, they came hunting for me. I tried to think of anything but my head, so I centered my thinking on the surroundings. We were heading northeast, going downhill at a comfortable stride. I figured by the foliage we'd dropped five or six hundred feet. Spruce pines and quaking aspen were thickly clumped and there were open parks. Spring buffalo grass stretched out for hundreds of acres. In the distance we'd sometimes see antelope. Once we crossed a shallow stream. A hundred yards away, a sow grizzly with two small cubs was sitting on a sand bar feeding on a buffalo that had washed downstream some time during runoff. Even at that distance, it made me a little nervous. A grizzly could outrun a horse in a short race. A she silvertip with cubs was nothing to get close to. The rugged peaks of the Wind Rivers were directly to our left. They were still heavily snowcapped and looked cold. Every now and then, I'd feel the rope tighten on my neck and glance over at the big Crow. The cruel expression on his lips never seemed to change. What I wouldn't give to slap that look off his face. I wanted to fight him in the worst way. There was no love lost between us, and I knew he was prodding me to see if I'd make a stupid move. It was more than just testing my courage. He was provoking me. Some people you meet and naturally dislike.

When the sun was almost directly overhead, we stopped. We'd worked our way down a steep trail to an open meadow. On the near side of the meadow were several enormous pines that would provide good shade in the summer and a windbreak in the winter. There was also a fair stretch of aspen that ringed the meadow on two sides. My head throbbed, but I worked at ignoring it. I was lucky to have hair. I dismounted by myself and did a miserable job, falling flat on my backside. It caused my head to smart in new ways. The braves found humor in it, but I could expect nothing less. It was their way to take pleasure in another's pain.

But I was Wolf Rockwell and I wasn't about to let this bunch get me off my horse if I could help it. I had my pride and my own code and I could live and die by it, too. This was a harsh land and only a tough people could make a life here. Still, there's nothing I would have changed. I wasn't so foolish as to think that someday it might not all be gone. Look what the Mormons did to the Great Basin. Get a bunch of farmers all working together and, before you know it, everything is tamed and good for nothing but farming and churches and schools. Farming is a good way of life, I suppose, but it's not my way. I'm a heathen and I like weeds. I like it wild. Knowing someone wants to lift my hair gives living an edge and a sweetness it wouldn't have otherwise, especially on a farm. However, under the circumstances, I was wishing things weren't quite this sweet. I'll be honest, I was wishing I was heading down the Green with my hides.

I knew it was best to be as little trouble as possible. Otherwise, if things got tight, I'd be the first item they'd cut themselves loose of, except for my hair. I knew what waited for me. But a man has hopes and to stay alive as long as possible was all I could expect.

I was picking up words and understanding more than I would have thought. Left Foot had taken up teepee living with a Crow squaw on the Yellowstone a few years ago. I learned as much of her language as I could. I was a little rusty since that had been a while ago, but I was catching on fast. I'd done some damage to their war party. I guess they liked the way I fought and that I'd taken the others out in hand-to-hand fighting. Indians set great store with stuff like that. They were taking me back to camp because I was a good omen. I guess the plainest way to say it is I was big medicine and was going to be the tribe's entertainment. They were going to see how brave I was. It was sure to be more pleasant for them than for me. But hell, I was alive, and I had to be grateful for that, at least I thought I should be. From their talking, I could tell they were from the Whistling-water clan and were camped near the Six Waters. Later they would join up with the Sore-lip clan for the spring buffalo hunts.

The braves let the horses feed on the lush green. The Crow with a brain-tanned buckskin shirt and grizzly necklace threw me a piece of jerky. He was a few inches shorter than Scar, older too. He was definitely in charge and he looked like he knew what he was doing. He wore leggings like Scar, but newer. Instead of a loincloth, he had the traditional elk-hide aprons, held in place by a white man's belt. A buffalo powder horn and a bag hung under his left arm. He was carrying a rifle.

I knew his name was Mighty Bear Claw. He didn't bother to cut the thongs that held my wrists. I ate that strip of jerky faster than a weasel eats eggs in the hen house. I was building up a powerful hunger and this wasn't going to do it. Many mountain men ate up to ten pounds of meat a day. It wasn't unusual to eat three or four pounds at a sitting, topped off with roast intestines cooked on a green stick over a fire.

After I'd eaten, if you could call it that, Mighty Bear Claw, who was holding the ropes around my neck, dropped the ends and signaled for me to drink in the stream twenty-five yards from where I sat. I noticed he carried the war pipe. Scar liked to throw his weight about, but on this raid he was just playing second fiddle, trying to be a war chief. The Crow had a fancy way of getting to be war chief, and then it was only a chief for a certain raiding party. Being a war chief was a complicated thing. A brave had to carry the sacred war pipe in battle. He had to steal a horse from an enemy. He had to take a war lance, a bow, or a rifle in hand-to-hand combat. And he had to count at least one coup where he touched an enemy directly. If he did this, he made good medicine and might be called on to be chief for a time or during a raid.

I plunged my head in the running water and drank. All along I was keeping my hands with those thongs under water, getting them as wet as I could. The drinking didn't kill my hunger, but it dulled the pangs. The thoughts of making a break entered my mind. I was sorely tempted to run for the nearest cover, which was a heavy clump of stately pines about a hundred yards off. My hands being tied didn't worry me much since a sharp rock would be all

I'd need. If I kept working at them, maybe they'd loosen up. Then I could slip out of them.

I was tempted. But they were watching me, and I knew it. They were playing a little cat and mouse. Let the white eyes run off and catch him because catching is fun. I might have dealt myself in, too, but my head was still throbbing and I wasn't sure how far I could trot before tumbling over. Back East I'd always been a fast runner. I took to running like Kentucky boys take to corn liquor. At rendezvous I nearly always won the foot races and picked up a new hawk or knife as a prize. Sometimes Left Foot would get the men together and place wagers. He gave me half. I liked to walk, too, unlike most mountain men who mostly rode a horse whenever they could. More than once I'd trotted at a steady pace, carrying my Hawken and possibles from dawn to dusk.

If I could make the trees, I'd have a chance. But I wasn't sure I'd get more than twenty yards before I lost my feet. I could feel the spot in the small of my back where Scar would aim his war lance. I'd risk it normally, I suppose. I was worried since a man gets so few chances to make a break with Crows. But I was too weak. I wanted to get my strength up before I made a break for it. That time would come . . . or I hoped it would.

We started moving again and the land got flatter. There were plenty of trees and I could see the mountains in the west. The braves rode with a sense of urgency. Mighty Bear Claw and Scar traded off holding my neck rope. That Bear Claw seemed like a fair man, and I respected him for the way he treated me. Scar was just water moccasin mean. He kept me in tight, almost shutting off my breathing. Several times he took pleasure, when we were on a rough part of the trail, pulling me backwards off my horse.

In the afternoon, riding down a steep draw, I had to lean back on my pony to keep my balance. It was steep and I wasn't used to riding without a saddle. I had a handful of mane, but it wasn't near enough with my hands tied. The trail was rocky and Scar was behind me. Just as I was trying to get my balance, he gave me a good tug. I rolled over the back of my pony and down the path until the rope went taut, choking my breathing air off.

I had to bide my time. That son of a striped skunk didn't slow down. He kept going, dragging me by the neck until I could get my feet under me. And I'll be danged if he didn't nudge his pony, speeding him up. We finally stopped at the top of a rise to look over a large spread of prairie and I managed to mount my horse. Several times he prodded me in the back with the blunt end of his war lance. It stung, but I was too mad to flinch.

I bit my lip and watched streaks of sweat form on Blue's flanks. I made a vow to myself right then. I would get Scar if it was the last thing I did. The images of how I'd kill him raised my spirits some and gave me renewed hope.

We rode until the sun was below the horizon. The last arrows of light were shooting up from the dying sun as the braves stopped for camp. The day had taken a toll on me. My head was spinning like a top, but mostly I was tuckered out. Exhaustion swept over me. Dinner was a handful of pemmican. The bear grease that held it together was turning rancid. I couldn't identify everything, but I knew there were mashed choke cherries mixed with powdered buffalo jerky. The Crows ate theirs with relish. After they were done, they divided up the last of my dried moose. I was as hungry as a schoolboy at a June picnic, and though I never could stomach pemmican under the best of conditions, I ate it this time. I don't much care for bear grease on a good day, let alone when it's turned. I was starting to feel myself again. My head still ached some, especially when someone pulled that rope and yanked me about like a dog. But I was getting my strength back.

When the sun had slipped beyond the mountains, it was cold. The wet ground had firmed up. Before too long, all the puddles and the still water by the creek would have ice. It was going to be chilly and my coat was on Scar. Bear Claw had started a fire. Mostly Indians build small fires so they can't be seen. But tonight they made it blazing, which was fine by me. The only thing I could figure was they were near their home and feeling comfortable. Scar and the other brave with the buffalo horns went about gathering wood. They brought in some downed aspen and a bunch of dead fall from the spruce thickets.

I knew I'd freeze to death if I had to lie on the ground as cold as it was getting. I worked loose plenty of dead grass and stuffed it into my shirt and pants for added warmth. It wasn't easy with my hands tied and my neck bound, but I wasn't about to freeze. I gathered more grass for my bed, along with some boughs from the thicket that bordered our backs. I could have made a proper bed if they'd let me go into the thicket with an ax or a tomahawk, but that wasn't likely. The Crows watched me with amazement.

I warmed myself near the fire as best I could, the thin blanket on my shoulders against the night cold. The front of me was too hot and the back was too cold. I'd half fallen asleep sitting there when Scar pulled me to the ground. He pointed at a place away from the fire and indicated that I should sleep. I arranged the boughs and clumps of grass as best I could. Hardly having the energy to chew the last of my jerky, I settled into my blanket with my feet and legs to the fire. It was a cold night. The wind picked up, hustled right through my clothes, and chilled me good. I used every trick I knew to stay warm. I pushed myself up and down with my elbows. I tightened up my muscles in my legs and rolled from side to side. It helped a little but not so I was comfortable. I dozed off only to wake shivering a little while later. I wanted to inch in to the fire, but they had me tied so I couldn't move more than a couple of feet.

I was grateful to see dawn arriving. When my wake-up kick came, I timed the movement and rolled with the blow before it struck. I hardly felt it. The braves built the fire and we warmed by it until the sun was above the horizon. The heat from the fire and the sun helped ease the pain in my aching body. Scar gave me a hard snap to get me moving.

It was too hard and I'd had enough. I grabbed the excess rope, jerking it out of Scar's his hand. Without thinking, I did something very foolish for a man in my situation. I doubled up that slack rope and slapped him on the cheek with it as hard as I could. I must have put power in back of it because it drew blood to his lips.

He drew his knife and came at me.

CHAPTER 4

I'll tell you this—a man coming at you with something pointed gets your blood warmed in a hurry! It was the first time I'd been warm since yesterday afternoon, but I wasn't enjoying it. I didn't want this piece of frozen ground to be the place I sucked in my last breath, nor did I fancy my chest being a sheath for Scar's hunting knife. I had to avoid the blade that was whipping back and forth like a snake's tongue. For that matter, I couldn't let Scar get a hold of the rope that was still attached to my neck. If I did, that would be the end since he'd pull me in like a catfish on a trot line.

The other braves backed up and let us fight. This was Scar's skirmish and he wouldn't have had it any other way. He'd lost face with his fellow braves and had to get it back honorably—which meant thumping on me. I turned my halter into a whip, the only weapon I could think of. Plunging to one side and dodging the knife sweeping toward my belly, I looked into Scar's face. His swelling lip still quivered. I took a long look into his eyes, eyes that were usually half closed. They were vacant, distant like the eyes of a someone walking a fine line between sanity and insanity. He lunged shrewdly, and when he did, I pounced back and brought my jury-rigged bullwhip swiftly down on his forearm. He lost his balance, but the blow didn't hurt anything more than his pride.

My forward motion had thrown off my footing, too, so I dropped to one knee to catch myself. My hand touched the ground and, instinctively, I had grabbed a handful of dirt before I jumped back up. I wanted to fight him. Now I was getting my chance. There was fire in his eyes when he came at me this time. He kept jabbing that blade, hoping to connect with something soft. Like a rattlesnake shedding its skin, he struck out blindly again and again at any sign of movement. It was an old knife fighter's trick to get me off balance. He was trying to scare me so I'd do something stupid or get me to thinking he could only make short jabs. He wanted me preoccupied with his knife—not with the man wielding it. I may not be the best knife fighter, but I didn't fall for it. I sort of pretended I was game in my right leg, moving like I favored it slightly. I was doing some trickery of my own. I didn't have much else since he had the blade.

He made a sudden lunge for my chest. I sidestepped his advance, but he tagged me. It wasn't a bad cut, but it bled. I hadn't moved quick enough. He had a jab as fast as a cat's paw. Scar tried the same move again but, when he came, I was ready. I heaved that handful of dirt into his eyes as he pounced. He brought his left hand up to clear his sight and, when he did, I brought that rawhide whip across his ribs with all my might. Then I whacked him again. It didn't sound loud, but the strap seemed to melt around his chest.

It knocked some meanness out of him, but I don't think it broke any ribs.

As he hunched forward, I tried a fancy kick I'd learned from a trapper called Frenchie Jock. He spent some time with us on the Green and could that fellow kick. I kept the rope in my hand, out of the way, and took a little hop forward to get into range. My right foot caught him under the jaw. I swore to myself I'd get even and I did. I gave it all the force I had. It snapped his head back, throwing him on the ground, stunned. Frenchie would have been proud. Then, with my left foot, I pinned his knife hand and snagged up the weapon by the blade.

He started to groan and I gave him one more kick in the groin, so he'd remember me. I'd not forgotten his kicks or that foolish neck rope. Then I kicked him again. The kick to the groin was as hard as I could muster and I heard laughter from the other braves.

Now, I wasn't a damn fool. I knew a man with a knife was no match for braves with rifles. As if I'd planned it, I walked as casually as you sit to the braves and handed Scar's Green River sticker to Bear Claw. Still carrying my own rope halter proudly, I drifted over to the pool for a long drink. I knew all eyes were upon me. I walked back and kicked Scar again. In my best broken Crow, I spoke to Mighty Bear Claw. I said that I was proud to be a brave and would not be treated like a common squaw. "Crow warriors," I said, "have taken me in battle after I had fought Crow braves in combat. Warriors must respect warriors," I went on. "Kill me if you will, but don't treat me like you'd treat a coward or a squaw."

I handed him my rope and told him I was his captive, for there was the honor of warriors between us. Between me and Scar there was only bad blood. The next time I would kill him. I'd enjoy fighting with him again. I think I gained respect from Bear Claw, and I was sure he'd treat me fairly.

The Crow chief took the rope and motioned for me to sit. He said something so fast I couldn't make it out, but Scar was glaring and smarting. I guess what I'd said worked, because the big Indian left me alone, although I could tell that nothing would please him more than to sink that scalping knife of his into my back. If I could read between the lines, I'd say he got his way most of the time. He wasn't used to getting whipped in a fair fight, especially by a mountain man with a rope on his neck.

Mighty Bear Claw walked to the stream and opened up a small bag. He mixed some powder with water, making a paste. Then he painted his face black, which the leader of a victorious war party always did before returning to camp. When he was done, the rest of the braves, even the one with the bad shoulder, blackened their faces. We mounted our horses and started off at a quick pace. We couldn't be far from their camp. The trail had gotten gentler, falling away into a long slope. It faded into an open stretch of tall prairie grass that came half way to my horse's belly. Scar seemed to be thinking about something else, at least he wasn't riding me for the moment. The afternoon sun felt warm and good on my shoulders, but they hadn't brought me this far for my health. I'd seriously hurt three braves—one had died. Then I'd humiliated Scar. I couldn't expect a box social. I'd never been here myself, but it looked like the Six Waters country some trappers had told me about. It was the place where the Crows moved each spring. There was a lot of tall grass so there'd be buffalo and the water was sweet to the taste.

By midmorning, as the sun was peeking out from behind the eastern clouds, we topped a rise. In a long valley there were forty-odd tepees. Mighty Bear Claw took the blanket he was wearing about his shoulders and swung it in the air seven times, probably the signal returning parties gave before riding into camp.

We waited.

In a few minutes, he did it again. His signal was answered by a guard who responded in kind. Although they were a long ways away, I could see folks scurrying in the village. This was an ideal place for a camp. I could think of none better. It was sheltered from the wind by a string of cottonwoods lining the banks of two clear creeks that joined together to make a larger stream. There was plenty of firewood and lots of sweet grass for the ponies. The spring grass grew thick and green. They'd obviously camped here many times before since heavy poles and brush were joined together to make a natural corral on three sides for their considerable string of horses. Crow raiding parties must have been successful, of late, with this many mounts. The front of the corral was roped off and several boys watched the herd.

Without much wind, the spring sun would warm the air nicely. The common space for meeting and socializing lay in the middle of the tepees. Green hides were spread out by the side. We dropped over the lip of a slight rise and started in. I wasn't looking forward to what was below. My stomach was getting tight and there was a tingling in my scalp and forehead. I had a strong desire to see what was over the next rise in the opposite direction. In fact, I wanted to see what was over any rise. I felt the rope on my neck and the bite of the thongs that bound my wrists.

The braves had come home with a captive. I knew that cruelty, as we whites might call it, was part of their life. War and raiding and death were with them every day. Bearing pain without complaint was what was expected of everyone, even children. As I'd learned when I first came to the mountains, torture among the tribes isn't a personal thing or something that comes from being evil-minded. Taking pain is an assumed virtue and a brave man must take it without comment. It would be to his shame if he didn't. A warrior captured in battle is proved great by how he bears torturing after the fighting is over. It's probably hard for a white man to understand, but it makes great sense in a Crow's way of thinking. If you're captured, you expect nothing less than the worst, and you're prepared to take what is dished out without complaint. In one sense, it's an indirect way of honoring a captive and celebrating his bravery beyond the battlefield.

Thinking about it didn't comfort me any. But I knew what to expect. It looked to me like I was about to get honored. Don't get me wrong, some white men aren't always living up to their Sunday school lessons, you can be sure of that. Still, cruelty, in general, runs against our God-fearing ways. We've had it drummed into us to look down on such behavior as uncivilized. In tea-party society or even in a humble sod-house kitchen, you'd never hear talk about quartering up a man or how loud a fellow might scream when someone started to skin him alive. You'd not discuss how many glowing coals you needed to stuff in a woman's mouth to send her heavenward. It wouldn't set well with lunch, and it might get God mad at you.

Still, for being so civilized ourselves, we've done some mighty wicked things to the redskins. And we're folks that are supposed to know better. We've got no room to talk—we even own slaves. How bad can that be? If what I'd learned about a thing called the Spanish Inquisition in the Middle Ages was true, some things were done in God's name that He couldn't have been too happy about. With an Indian, being what we call cruel is part of his way of looking at life. Being mean with us, though, is supposed to run against our civilized grain. But we do it anyway.

Without warning, Scar slipped up behind me, took that lead from Bear Claw's hand, and took off at a dead run for the village, yelling and whooping. He led me along like his pet dog. It was all I could do to hang on, my hands being tied up. Didn't take much to see that he was trying to unseat me from my horse. I tried to keep behind him but Blue didn't turn fast enough. I felt myself starting to fall so I let go of the mane and reached up for the rope, since I'd choke to death otherwise.

I grabbed it high and worked my hands up the rope as I was in mid air. Even though I hit the prairie with a hard thud, I knew I couldn't let go. A crowd had gathered to watch the excitement—me being paraded through the village. It was common to display the fruit of a successful raid, but I never thought I'd be that fruit. With dust in my mouth and eyes smarting, I hoped there weren't any large rocks to make my afternoon worse. The dogs in the village took up the chase, nipping at my heels and yelping up a frenzy. On the edge of the village, Scar turned for another pass which gave me time to get a better hold on the rope before he showed me off some more.

As he kicked his horse, the rope went tight. I supposed this would be a good time to start praying for some help. I hit a bump and was shot upward before I could think further on it. I crashed to the ground like a glass hitting a stone floor. While being dragged at a full gallop, I didn't pay much attention to the people screaming and throwing rocks or to the pack of semi-wild curs eager to sink their fangs into my calves. I fixed my attention to hanging on to that rope so I could live to be tortured.

After he'd drug me back and forth a few times, Scar stopped in the middle of the tepees. I knew I was in more trouble than I'd bargained for but at least my personal excitement was over for the moment. There was howling and wailing over by the horses carrying back the wounded. One young squaw's grief was especially bad. Her brave must have been the one who had died of his wounds. All this sorrowing gave me a chance to catch my breath and spit the dust out of my mouth. I noticed that several braves never took their eyes off me. Scar's lip was still quivering. I got the feeling Mighty Bear Claw was the only thing keeping him from sending me to my own Happy Hunting Ground. During long winters and at rendezvous, I'd heard plenty about what Crow like to do. And I have to tell you, it made my flesh crawl to think about it. They've got more nasty ways of making hurt than a man has time to experience in a few dozen lives.

The thing you have to do, the old timers used to say, was be brave and fight back. "Your only hope," Hatchet Jack used to drawl, "was escaping, if you got lucky. Your other choice is getting them braves to kill you fast . . . provoke them to kill you in anger so you don't suffer much."

Course, I'd rather escape if it was all equal. Maybe in an hour or two I'd be wishing Scar had run me through this morning. If escaping didn't work, and it didn't seem likely, I'd make Scar mad enough to end my days fast. Some might have said I was a fool back on the trail, fighting him back. Some might say I ought to have let him sink that hunting knife in my chest, get it over without a fuss. Fighting back, though, not giving up, was the Rockwell way.

We like a fight. My ancestors were some of the first to shed blood in the Revolutionary War. I guess they didn't like being told what to do any better than me. I had a great uncle who was at the Boston Tea Party. Another kinsman took a ball in 1812. And if what Orin told me was right, and I haven't cause to doubt him, there were a few others who spent time in the stocks for speaking out.

Maybe it was the healthy dose of proud Irish blood that flowed in my veins. To flee some tyrant landlords like the British, we Irish men took off to all parts of the world, fighting across Europe. There wasn't much else, besides fighting, for us to do. There was little opportunity as it was. Soldiering was the best way to get a stake and come back and start a new life. We were good at fighting and liked the sting of battle. Most of all we hated bullies, and we weren't good at giving in even if it made life hard on us.

I couldn't roll over like a possum in the backwoods, not while there was still a chance. I'm not one of those men who thinks his number won't turn up, though. I know it could happen and it will sooner or later. If it weren't Indians, it could be walking into an ornery griz, getting caught in a blizzard, having my horse fall and break my leg. Could be a number of things. I don't dwell on it, but I know it could happen. But I'll always keep fighting until my last breath.

The noise had calmed down a little and something caught my attention. The women and the kids were forming two lines, and I knew what would be coming next. The tea kettle was about to boil over.

I was about to run the gauntlet.

Chapter 5

Just because squaws and young folks make up this game, it doesn't mean there's no cause for some major worry. Some captives never live long enough to get a turn with the braves according to Left Foot Bill and the old timers on the Green.

Being turned completely over to the women, however, was a fate reserved for a man they considered a coward or one who didn't handle himself well in battle. The squaws might beat and kick you without mercy, then proceed with dull knives. Sometimes it took a captive two days to die slowly. It was a bad way to cash in. I knew from over-hearing some conversations, I was being warmed up.

The village folks were picking up whatever was handy. The stories I'd heard weren't just campfire yarns. A withered old crone to my left hefted a buffalo leg bone half as tall as she, not wanting to miss the fun. Another clenched a weathered rawhide quid. A boy about twelve grabbed up a handy piece of firewood as thick as his wrist. Two children were sharpening sticks on a rock. Others picked up stones. One young squaw, the one who'd been crying, had a rusty butcher knife clutched in her bloody fist.

The object of this game was to stick or hit the runner, which in this case was me, inflicting as much pain as possible. Everyone would get their turn, too. And if the runner fell, which was a bonus, they ganged up and beat or clubbed or stabbed him within an inch of his life. They had to leave something for the braves to play with.

The line formed quickly. There were about thirty or more volunteers and they stood in two lines. I knew those lines would tighten up once I got moving and the crowd got excited about clubbing me. "The trick," Frenchie had said one evening as he was charging his pipe, "is to keep going as fast as ye can. Ya' got one chance and that's to keep motion a' working for ya', never slowin' it down. If ya' do fall down, you're just about done far. If ye roll into a ball and play dead, they might lose interest, especially after you've quit breathing."

It didn't seem funny, now.

I walked toward them. Those who'd been wailing and sorrowing the most were at the front, like that pretty young squaw. Her name was Mountain Flower, if I'd heard correctly, and she was eager with that rusty sticker. Her legs were all bloody from self-inflicted gashes, which was the Crow woman's way of mourning when her man had been killed or hurt bad. Her buckskin dress was stained red brown. She broke out into another uncontrollable fit of hysterics, digging the point of that blade into her thigh to punctuate her sorrow one more time. She stared up at me like a hound at a treed coon and screamed. Fresh blood had soaked through the clotted crust of her dress and was dripping from her fingertips.

She'd have looked a lot prettier with something else in her hand, I'll tell you that. I couldn't see what most were carrying because of the way they were crowded in and it was just as well. Maybe I could get past that woman with the rusty knife who had already practiced using it on herself. About twenty feet from the front of the line, I stopped and beat my chest. Indians love a good show and I was going to give them one.

I had nothing to lose at this point.

I looked at Mighty Bear Claw who seemed to be in charge of the afternoon's entertainment. I pointed to him respectfully and spoke in a loud voice so the others would hear. I said I was named *Mighty Wolf*, after the greatest wolf on the prairie. I told him I was pleased to test my courage and prayed the Crows would strike hard blows so I could prove my bravery. That way I could be honored as a warrior. I looked into the sky and chanted the only Latin phrase I'd learned, stuff I'd tried to forget when I was in school.

I couldn't remember what it meant, but I started singing it louder and louder, running in a tight circle, raising and lowering my head as I did. I was almost shouting when I stopped and fell to my knees. I grabbed two handfuls of dirt, sifting it slowly into the soft breeze. I sang a few verses of "Come, Come Ye Saints," a Sunday school song Mormons were so fond of. I got the words wrong, but they'd never know. I acted brave, but my throat was dry and my palms were wet.

I addressed the sun and sky in my best Crow, hoping it would buy me time. I removed that leather rope from my neck, dropping it at my feet. I jumped about again, spouting off the Latin phrase. Not wanting to give the line any warning, I darted as fast as I could for the opening, shouting and howling my best war whoops. My hope was to come in so rapidly that I could get part way through before they knew it. I didn't fancy that rusty knife much, and Mountain Flower looked like a squaw who was more than willing to punch it in me. I'd whipped her man in battle and she'd like to get even so he could rest easier in the world of spirits.

It worked. I got five or six feet into the line before I felt the first blow. It was a heavy one, but I kept low and put my hands ahead of me. The line closed in around me and I was lost in a sea of bodies, heavy blows, and bad air. It was hard to breathe and the air became stale and rancid. I lost track of anything but pushing. My only thought was to survive this cute little game.

When they got too close, I pushed harder and hurt back. If I got lucky, some Crow might get punished by her own in these tight quarters. I won't say their blows didn't hurt, because they did. But it wasn't as bad as I'd thought, at least not yet. Keep moving, I told myself. I started shoving hard and pushing. Being slow meant taking extra punishment. Never give them a chance to get a second blow or poke, I told myself.

My back took most of the abuse. This wasn't a new game to some of them. A few tried to trip up my footing. If they got me to fall, it got more interesting. Well, more interesting for them. It sure wouldn't be for me.

Someone threw a fist-size rock. I saw a boy jab me with his spear and felt it bite my leg. A heavy object that felt like an iron frying pan brushed against my back. I kept on, anyway. Wrestling and hard work had made my back strong. I respect women mind you and wouldn't hit a child under normal circumstances, but I was letting loose with both barrels pushing bodies this way and that, just so they didn't fall in front of me. I was giving a few blows myself as I went. It be me or them and I was more worried about me.

A brave joined the fun, standing toward the end. I could see light beyond him. I ducked toward him and thrust my head between his legs. Grabbing his knees, I jerked him off the ground as I stood. I started swinging as fast as I could. He wasn't a large man so I had little trouble. As I was swinging him about, the crowd naturally cleared. Some, in their zeal to thump me, gave him some punishment instead. I pitched him about a few more times and let him go. He felled three squaws, scattering them like lawn pins. They never knew what hit them.

I made it to the end of the line and ran off a few yards. I let out a big howl and another war whoop. I jumped up and down, beating my chest again. I was bloody, but I didn't think anything was broken, least not so I could tell. Most of the cuts, I hoped, were shallow. My leg was bleeding where the kid had shoved his stick. I didn't take time to check further, but I did something they didn't expect.

Since I had nothing to lose, I shouted and whooped some more, plunging back into the line and working my way up again. It was easier this time. The brave I'd thrown had disoriented a few more women and children, and I got past the first group with only a few light blows. By the time I got into the middle, they were again at me in earnest. My back and legs felt like a pincushion at a quilting bee. But this time they weren't as eager to get close. They'd discovered I had teeth. I swerved to one side or another, running into some, avoiding others. I plowed into some teenage girls, so several others standing nearby let me pass.

One squaw let loose with a well-timed piece of deadwood and hit me in the back of the head. I started to see a few stars but I kept moving. By the time I neared the end of my beating line, I saw the woman with the knife crouched ready to spring. She stepped in front of me with her blade raised. She'd planned for me to be bent low like I'd been, so I turned toward her standing up. I raised my arm, deflecting her blow. I caught her wrist and twisted hard. She fell backward.

I kept running, but the last of the line opened up and let me through. I noticed that the tribe was shouting and cheering, too. I'd brought them honor and helped vindicate the braves I'd fought. Their warriors had, indeed, been whipped by a worthy foe. It was an honor, in their way of thinking, to be taken out by a brave man who proved himself. Truth be told, I wasn't all that mighty, just plain scared. But I didn't know what else to do. As long as they thought I was mighty, I'd have some breathing time to form some sort of plan.

Several braves with long, sharp points on their lances, along with Might Bear Claw, led me to a tepee. The first brave went in the opening that faced east. Indians were funny about the way they set up their lodges. They always have their doors facing east. A brave they called Dull Horn (he'd been on the raid) motioned abruptly for me to sit. Dull Horn and Mighty Bear Claw sat in the sacred part of the tepee directly opposite the door and across the fire—a place no captive would be allowed to occupy. The other braves sat on the sides.

The buffalo hide was nice and soft, first comfortable thing I'd been on in a while. The Crow were known for how they dressed a buffalo robe. A small fire burned in the middle. The tepee felt comfortable, smelling of half-burned buffalo chips, dried grass, and smoked hides. Of all the plains tribes, Crows have the largest tepees, taking almost twenty buffalo skins for the walls. This one was about eighteen feet across and used fourteen poles at least twenty feet high.

Bear Claw called out and a middle-aged squaw with streaks of gray in her hair brought in a wooden bowl of boiled buffalo meat. She wore a long dress of deer hide, tanned white. She had soft, knee-high leggings, and moccasins trimmed with quill. She must have been an important woman in the tribe since she was wearing a hundred elk teeth, which were considered precious.

I held the bowl she handed me as carefully as a mother holds a new born. I drank the warm broth, lingering over each drop. I felt strength coming back to my cut-up body, chewing each piece of tender meat slowly, drawing out the juices. I ate the contents of the bowl, paying little attention to anything else. I needed strength. It tasted good after almost three days with nothing but a few handfuls of jerky and pemmican. If only I had a pot of coffee to top it off and a big slice of dried-apple pie.

After I was done eating, I looked up at the braves. Mighty Bear Claw was armed only with a knife, but I couldn't help looking at Dull Horn. He looked about my age, maybe a little older. He'd kept busy by the looks of things. I wondered if he planned on my hair hanging from that lance as well. In a few words of broken English, mixed with sign and Crow, Bear Claw told me I had honored his tribe with bravery, something rare for a white man. I bowed my head slightly to acknowledge and he continued. He said to rest. Later I would test the courage and bravery of his young warriors, the warriors who weren't seasoned in battle.

When he left, two braves stayed, quietly watching me.

Mrs. Rockwell didn't raise any fools. Since I'd just eaten, and the robe was soft and the tepee warm, I turned my back and went to sleep. My leg was hurting some and my back was a bit stiff, but when I laid my head on that hide, my eyes just shut and I was out like a baby.

It seemed but an instant later I was awakened by the butt of a war lance prodding me in the back and not gently either. They weren't doing all this feeding and letting me sleep because they were running a fancy hotel. They were taking care of me the way you'd take care of a pit bull or a fighting rooster. They wanted to keep me healthy so I could fight.

I was led out by Dull Horn, the one who had waked me. He led me to a flat spot outside of camp. The grass had all been trampled down. In the center a stake three feet high and as thick as a man's wrist had been driven into the ground. It was more a short pole than a stake, really. Apparently we were going to play a version of what the mountain men call *Man-at-the-Stake* and the man was me.

Chapter 6

A brave tied my neck rope to the top of the stake and handed me a thick stick a little less than two feet long. The young braves, six of them, divided into pairs. Each carried a club. Theirs were longer and slightly heavier than the one I was handed. They'd smeared charcoal on their faces until it was as thick as Mississippi mud and I could hardly tell their features.

I knew this game, having played it myself with other mountain men at rendezvous. The only difference was we tied the man to the stake by the waist, not the neck. We also wrapped our clubs with a generous amount of rabbit fur so no one got badly hurt when you clubbed them hard. Sometimes we played in pairs, other times we played it one on one.

The object was to get the man tied to the stake, knock him down, and then punish him with a few well-timed blows. He couldn't move further than the rope, so the attacking men had the advantage. If the man on the lead got taunted into chasing too far, the lead would knock him off his feet when he came to the end. The other attacker could come in and get him. At the rendezvous, we took turns being roped. I doubted we'd switch off today.

I was feeling good. I'd had some food and rest, and I was, in a strange sort of way, looking forward to this. I did a few squats to help get the stiffness out, touching my toes, hoping to get the blood moving in my back. I hefted my hitting stick again, finding the best place to grip it. I swung it through the air savagely. I loosened the lead on my neck a might when I didn't think anyone was looking. Then I loosened it up a little more. Next I walked around the stake and made a mental note about how far I could go in a circular direction. I noted clods and rocks to mark the stopping point. I'd found when you take a cuff you want to dish one back. It's easy to overstep the lead and find yourself flat. The secret to this game was to stay close to the pole. I drew a mental ring about the stake at about half my lead. I'd try not to go farther. I tucked some of the rope into my waistband so it wouldn't get in the way of my swinging. It would also give me a little warning if I went too far and it came out.

Bear Claw raised his hand and started to chant the ancient warrior's song taught to all young men entering manhood. It was a prayer of sorts to be brave. It went close to this:

> *Old age is a hateful thing. Look to danger!*
> *Charge into the enemy. Look to danger!*
> *Old age is evil. Look to danger!*
> *The stars and sun are ceaseless. Look to danger!*
> *The earth is eternal as are you. Look to danger!*
> *Face the enemy undaunted. Look to danger!*

Two young boys, one might have been fifteen, the other sixteen, came at me in a mad rush. They were looking to danger, all right. The youngest boy came in impulsively, as he'd been taught. It was the warriors' creed to be brave, so dying young was an honorable thing, as long as you demonstrated you had courage. This thinking couldn't help but make a young warrior reckless. This one was too anxious. He'd been taught that growing old was a burden to the tribe. From an early age, bravery and skill in battle were the focus of his life. He had the heart of the warrior, but not the skill. He charged right in with the grace of a rutting bull moose in thick willows.

Guess he'd not played this game much. Instead of working as a team, having one decoy while the other held back until the tied man opened himself, these two were fighting individually. The gospel fact was they were working against each other, giving me the upper hand because of it. The youngest brave, wanting to make a quick score and a big coup, suddenly came in fast, his braids flying in the air behind him. He held his club waist high until he got within striking range.

Yes, he was brave, I'll give him that. But he wasn't smart. Unless he sharpened up his skills, he'd not live past his first raid. The other boy was holding off to the side, not coming in as much. He was unsure of what to do. His false charges were bluffs, easy to read. The reckless one came in and it was too easy. I never moved, I just brushed him aside and pushed him head first into the pole, which put him out cold as stunned fish. The other boy should have come at me right then, but he held back, still not sure how to approach. Keeping a weather eye on him anyway, I bent down and grabbed the unconscious kid by the scruff of the neck and flung him out of my circle. I didn't want to trip on him or have him come to and get me from behind.

He was pulled back and cared for by a brave.

I believe the best defense is to attack and keep going. But I've never been sure if it's worse to attack too eagerly or hold back like my old granny, waiting for the right time. This young brave couldn't make up his mind how to come at me, so he mostly loitered just out of my reach. I stood there and taunted him, getting him in range. In this game it's supposed to be the other way around.

I gave him the time of day, cursing him randomly. He finally charged me wildly like I'd insulted his mother, which I might have. His club was swinging crazy-like over his head. I blocked his first blow easily which threw his timing off. As he stumbled, he dropped his arms to catch his balance. When they came down, I cudgeled the arm that held his weapon with a full swing.

It broke under my blow.

Taking his club, I turned him about and nudged him back into the crowd with the back of my foot. He never whimpered, but he was in pain as he stumbled off. I admired his mettle but not his fighting technique. Unlike white boys, Crows were taught in the ways of battle from when they were knee high to mule deer. These two were learning that real battle was a harsh schoolmaster. Like the prayer Bear Claw chanted, boldness and courage was the only path to honor while old age was evil. It was drummed into them how fine it was to die in battle. Of course I sorely disagreed with that philosophy since I hoped to be a ripe old age, which wasn't looking too promising at the moment. Dying in battle just wasn't my way. You could say I wanted to live in battle. I hoped I'd be brave, but dying wasn't nearly as splendid as living . . . or dancing a jig with a pretty girl or watching the evening sun set in the peaks.

I waited for the next pair to come at me.

The next two were signaled. They charged at once. They weren't much better, but at least they both came in at me, rather than one holding out. I sent both back to their people anyway. I supposed I'd honored them with broken bones, sore heads, and battle experience. It seemed a rough way to grow up. But it was their way, and I wasn't about to change it. I felt bad about what I did to these lads, but I'd no choice about my invitation to this party. At least these boys could keep their pride since none had turned tail and run. They could wear their scars proudly.

The last two I fought were different. They were older and more seasoned. One was very good and I was worried. They'd been at this game before and they came in carefully circling about. I hugged the back of the pole for protection. Then both charged at once, but from opposite sides. I had to watch them both out of the corner of my eyes since each was trying to come in on both my blind sides. I knew there was no way I'd get out of this without taking a few hard hits. I let my concentration slip just for a second and that was all one brave needed. I'd let myself focus on the swinging club of the brave to my right as he false charged. While my head was turned, the other brave snuck in and got a hold of my rope. Before I knew it, I was on my back blocking blows. The crowd had gone wild with cheering.

At least I had two sticks. I kept one up to protect my face while I tried to parry with the other. I stood up, groping for the rope with my left hand as a brave gave a strong pull that yanked me forward. I felt a blow on my back as I fell again. The braves were dancing about me and jeering, responding to the reaction on the sideline. One brave got in close and I rolled to whack him in the shins as he jumped out of the way. While they were taking bows and enjoying the appreciation of the congregation, I struggled back to the pole. I tucked a generous portion of rope into my waistband so I wouldn't outrun it and get floored. I'd have to be more careful.

If they got a hold of that rope again, I was sunk. They'd had their fun taunting me, but the next time I was on the ground, I could expect serious blows. I'd already had one to my head a few days ago, so I wasn't ready for another. I didn't fancy a broken bone either.

Like wolves, they came. I twisted and turned like a hand-caught trout trying to keep them off balance, working in strikes of my own. I took a solid blow in the side and another in the thigh. I needed a good lick on one of them to slow up the pace. I was wearing down fast. I held my clubs part way up the handles on purpose so they'd not know my real reach. They both came in. I parried the first blow, but I left myself open and took a jab in the stomach that knocked most of the wind out of me. I leaned back into the post to catch my breath. They were experienced and by now, knew my reach and stayed just outside.

They were at me again, pushing in, gauging how far I could strike. One charcoal-faced brave, with a bone breastplate, came in swinging, reaching for my rope. All the while the crowd was cheering and rooting for their village fighters. That noise made him more daring and he inched in closer, swinging that club, me blocking it at every turn. I was struggling to catch my breath.

The one with the breastplate had a need to prove how brave he was. He backed out and said something to the other. Whatever he said, the other attacker backed off a little, giving him space, which was just fine. He came in alone. He was tough, but at least I didn't have to glance over my shoulder or worry about getting tagged from behind.

This gave me a little breathing room. Breastplate was getting rather daring because he could see I was out of breath. When he was in close, he swung recklessly and I ducked. I grabbed as far back on my club as I could, giving me a larger reach, swung for all I had, and missed. Good thing for me he was paying attention to the cheering because I left myself open. He dove at me, trying to get my feet. It was unexpected, but I slid out of his way. The edge of his club just brushed my leg. He got up and feigned a few times.

He charged again but was too late with his swing. He brought up his club to protect his face against my returning blow. I hit lower than I'd meant and smashed across his knuckles. He was one warrior who wouldn't be holding a knife until fall. I caught him along his ribs and shoulder. He spun about, and I gave him a half-hearted swat on the back. He yelled out and fell over. His companion, who should have come at me since I was winded, yelled something. I assume it was Crow cussing. He drug his friend out. I let him go while I took some deep breaths and eyed the situation.

This brave had called me for his own, so the other fellow had let him have at me. I suppose it was greater honor if he took me alone. A little praise from the crowd had made him punch drunk. Should have spent more time worrying about fighting and less time enjoying the limelight until after I was beaten to a pulp.

The second brave lunged at me with a vengeance, mad as a mule with a burr in his saddle blanket. Diving to the side, he made a grab at my rope. He missed, but barely. He turned and came again without pausing, as if the honor of the clan rested in his hands alone. I lunged, and he blocked. Dropping the club in my left hand, I hit him in the breadbasket with my left, then again. He brought his club down, but I clutched his wrist to check the strike and locked my right forearm about the back of his neck. He'd done some wrestling, and he stopped my attempt to throw him over my shoulder. He was strong. If it weren't for the rope about my neck, I'd have been more eager for a ruff and tumble.

I couldn't budge him over my shoulder, so I turned as he tried to slam his knee into my groin. I had a mountain lion by the tail. If I let go, he'd have me. If I held on, he'd have me for sure. I was getting more and more tired. I feigned throwing him over my shoulder. He countered, expecting my drive to come from the top. I dropped down to my back, thrusting my compressed right foot into his belly. I sent him over my head without ceremony. He landed in a pile about five feet away, stunned. It gave me time to get to my feet, my clubs into position.

We fought for another five minutes, exchanging heavy blows and looking for the other's weakness. A good fighter has to bide his time, but this one got anxious. Otherwise he would have taken me since I was played out. He should have worn me down more, then made his move when I got careless. A wise warrior knows when to strike—no use taking punishment if you can wear your opponent out first.

I'd not want to face this one in a few years, but like many inexperienced fighters, he got confident when he saw me try to catch my breath. He came in fast and low, focused only on giving me the business end of his stick. He was watching me and lost his footing and his club when he tripped.

This fall was a lucky break and probably the only thing that saved me.

Before he had a chance to move, I was on him. I brought my club down as if to strike his neck. Since he had fallen on his side, it would have been a fatal strike. But I pulled it at the last moment bringing the club so it just rested across his neck.

Then I let him up.

Turning to Bear Claw I said, "These young warriors have done me a great honor. They are brave. Their courage pleases me. I thank you and their fathers and mothers. Those who live will be mighty braves, braves I hope to meet again in battle some day."

Dull Horn took the rope off my neck and led me back to the lodge.

Mighty Bear Claw sat in the sacred part of the tepee, smoking. I was directed to the same buffalo robe as before, and I'd never been more ready to sit down. Beside him was a stone-headed war club with a handle longer than my arm. It gave me shivers to think about facing a weapon like that. Besides being used for killing men, the Crow used it on the heads of wounded buffalo, splitting their skulls open like ripe watermelons.

The lodge was comfortable; the buffalo robe was soft. I was tired as a mule after spring plowing. Through lazy puffs of smoke, he looked at me in silence. We were on different sides of the war pipe, but there was an unspoken bond between us, the bond of warriors. I might have to kill him, or he me, but that wouldn't change our mutual regard. I would like to know him under different circumstances so we could ride together.

A solid man, Bear Claw was living true to his way, honoring the gifts the Great Spirit had given him. He lived in an untamed time, that's true, but he wasn't the wild ignorant savage some Eastern folks would have you think. His practices were no more uncivilized than those of the Greeks or Romans we esteem so much in school primers. The Crows were educated and schooled in the ways of the Plains—learning how to ride, hunt, make war. There was nothing about living off the land they didn't know. It took a lot of training to live out here. In Bear Claw's world there was honor, bravery, and tradition. He provided unselfishly for his family and his tribe through hunting and raiding. When necessary, he'd take up the war pipe and be a leader, even if it meant his blood. These folks followed the herds of buffalo and, because of the horse, they could kill the fattest animals and most of the time lived well. It was a good way, and I respected it.

As much as it pained me to admit it, I could see it was all changing. The Crows couldn't know it yet, but it was. People in the East were moving out into the frontier like ants after spilt honey. The other change began when the first trappers started bartering, tempting Indians with things they couldn't make themselves. Where they used to be all on their own, they'd become dependent upon trade goods like knifes, blankets, powder, lead, rifles, and cloth. Such truck would contribute to their undoing.

The flap opened and a young squaw brought in a bowl of boiled buffalo tongue and wild turnips. I knew I was being paid an honor since this dish was a delicacy. I drank the rich broth first. Buffalo makes a fine soup and there's nothing better. I picked out the turnips with my fingers and ate them slowly. Besides beans, these were the first vegetables I'd had all winter. And while I hated farming, I dearly loved what a handy vegetable garden can provide. The tongue had been sliced, and I ate each piece with pleasure.

When I was done, she took the wooden bowl and filled it again. For the first time in days, my stomach was content. My muscles were still aching some, and it smarted if I touched my leg where I'd been poked by that stick. My head was healing, but I could still feel the goose egg.

After I ate, Mighty Bear Claw spoke to me in simple Crow, trader English, and sign. I didn't know I'd picked up as much as I had from Left Foot's squaw. I couldn't speak it much, but if it was spoken to me slow, I could make it out. When I didn't understand, I just held up my hand, and he'd try telling me another way. It was slow going, but we communicated. At first he asked if I was full. I nodded my head; he puffed on his pipe.

In the Crow fashion, he told me I'd honored myself through bravery and that I'd honored his tribe and the warriors I had killed in battle. He told me that I was different from most white men since I understood the Indian ways and did not fight against them. Then, in a manner as serious and as deliberate as a hanging judge, he told me that the next day when the sun was at the highest point in the sky, I'd have a chance to win my freedom if I wasn't killed. He said only the bravest men were allowed this test and that he saw me as a brave man who had been brought by Great Spirit.

A warrior was only mighty if he did battle with mighty men. There was no glory or honor in doing battle with weak, cowardly men or women. His notion of honor and battle reminded me of knights and all that Round Table stuff. It wasn't so bad to be killed by a brave man. It was an even greater honor if you killed one.

He was likely sending me off to my blood letting, but he was nice about it. I might have a chance, although a small one, of getting out of this with my skin and hair. Even though Mighty Bear Claw was dressed in buckskins, for my two-bits he was just as much a gentleman as one of those rich Virginia planters.

At noon tomorrow, I would be fighting for my life and freedom.

I would run against the arrow.

Chapter 7

The sun had been up for some time before I awoke. I was aware of dogs barking and children playing. I'd almost forgotten where I was, the thick buffalo robe was so soft and inviting. I dozed for just a moment and rose up with a start. It was mid morning and I was in a tepee. I'd slept over fourteen hours.

My head felt clear. I was sore, but rested. My back was tender after being the backstop for every rock and piece of wood near camp. Sleep and food were the best medicines a man could ask for. I'm not one for sleeping past light, but it wasn't as if I could go anywhere. I was exhausted. There wasn't a guard inside the lodge, but I'd bet my uncle's farm there were a few braves who never strayed far from the outside. Someone must have heard me stirring about since the flap of the tepee opened. She carried the same roughly carved wooden bowl. It was filled with some sort of meat, probably antelope, and what I think was cattail roots. It wasn't as good as the dinner I'd eaten last night, but I ate it gratefully.

I'd need my strength before this day was over. Maybe I'd have an opportunity to escape, even if it was mighty slim. Figured my chances were about as good as a fox in a foxhunt. I wasn't complaining, mind you. The fox did get a head start. It beat being killed outright any day.

After I'd rested and thought a while, a squaw with a striking tattoo running from the edges of her lips to her chin brought in water. I drank deeply. I was starting off healthy. I couldn't help staring at her tattooed face when she came to pick up the bowl. Besides the tattoo about her mouth, I could see she had a circle on her forehead and a small circle on the tip of her nose. She was some sort of mystic in the clan since only a small number of special women had this done. The squaw Left Foot carried had been tattooed like this woman.

It must have hurt. To apply a tattoo she had to lie very still for hours. Then someone with a small clump of porcupine quills jabbed down on her skin, making a series of small punctures. Next, a light powder of pine tree and red willow ash was rubbed in. The process was repeated again and again until the design was made. Women usually had face tattoos, while men were tattooed on their arms and chests, sometimes the neck.

I lay down again, but it wasn't much use trying to rest. I couldn't sleep any more and I was uneasy. You try not to think about dying too much, but the thought creeps in anyway when you don't want it to. I thought of maybe someday settling down and having a family. I wanted a cabin I could call my own in the mountains, maybe with a piece of bottomland for a garden and a clear stream to sit by or fish in. I wanted to learn to read better and get a sack full of books to read through. Maybe I'd study for the law someday—maybe I'd run a few cows and a large string of mountain-bred horses. I knew I'd want a son to carry on my name when I was dust.

Of course at this point I'd be happy to see the sun rise on the Green River with my friends.

I couldn't let myself get double minded since I was about to run for my life. I'd give it all I was worth. This was a favorite way of testing a man. Mighty Bear Claw said he'd shoot the arrow himself and pick six braves to chase me. Between me and that stuck arrow would be free running. When I got to it, the chase began in earnest with the braves trying to run me down. After that I was free to run wherever I wanted. It was smart to remember you had a bunch of eager braves on your tail trying to overtake you. One only needed to get close enough to put their spear through you. They had the advantage of knowing the territory, so it wasn't good thinking to try and find a place to hide if you got out of sight. Never mind that they knew the hiding places and it was hard to mask a trail when you were followed that closely; usually, though, they'd keep you in sight. If you did manage to get away from them, they'd surely follow your sign. In fact, it added to the fun and excitement if they didn't get you right away. Following trails was what they did best.

The run was weighted in favor of the followers but my plan was simple. I wanted them to think I was more roughed up by all the fighting than I was. Maybe they'd get a little careless. Running had always come easy for me, so I felt I was on equal ground. I wanted to put distance between me and the warriors. At high noon they came. Mighty Bear Claw was with them. He called for another bowl of water and commanded me to follow him. We walked toward the edge of camp where the horses were kept. By the edge of the corral I noticed my truck stored with the Crow's tack. My furs, saddle, and one of my rifles were sitting in the corner of the brush hut. Besides being a place to store their equipment, the hut allowed the boys who watched the ponies to take shelter from the rain or hot sun.

We went a little farther to the edge of a small, clean stream. We were followed by most of the Indians in the village since this was a big event. I guess I was a major entertainment. A couple of braves came up behind me and ripped off my shirt. Another cut off my moccasins. This was something I hadn't planned for. By the stream, five braves were standing impatiently, wanting to start. The brave with the longest spear was Scar. Another was the young brave wearing buffalo horns, known as Dull Horn.

Scar's wanting to kill me so badly would give him extra endurance. He had something to prove and nailing my hide to the wall would erase the shame I'd brought him in his tribe's eyes. He glared at me through half closed slits, but I ignored him. The other warriors looked to be in good shape. I had my work cut out. Being barefoot would be a disadvantage, but when you are running for your life, you aren't going to notice the odd pebble or thorn. As long as I was trotting across the prairie grass, I'd be fine. When I headed into the woods or on rocks that might be a different story.

There wasn't much ceremony. The sun gave no shadow and there was a light breeze from the south. Across the creek, the large park spread out for a mile or so until it started to slope up, broken by low rolling hills partly covered with aspen and pine. To the west were the snowcapped mountains we'd ridden out of. Mighty Bear Claw drew an arrow out of his beaver-hide quiver and shot it in the air. It went about four hundred yards directly away from us to the southwest. I was nudged none too softly. I assumed this was my signal to start the race. Bear Claw and I exchanged a glance and I was off.

I fought my first impulse which was to run like a scared rabbit—which is what I felt like. In this situation it was easy to get excited for a chance at freedom and start off too fast. The secret, if there was one, was pacing yourself so you don't get played out. I started at a slow trot, favoring my leg, a favorite trick of mine, ambling across the park toward the arrow like someone who was hurt.

Truth was, I felt great. Stretching my legs felt good, but I still couldn't help feeling like the bird at an old fashion turkey shoot. My plan was to save my strength for later. It was my guess those braves, when I reached the arrow, would come off for all they were worth, each eager to be the first to throw his spear. By the way I was running, they'd think they could catch me easily. At least I hoped they would. If they didn't pace themselves, they'd get winded before long and I could put some distance between us. Then they'd have to work to make up the difference. I had to stay ahead. I'd need all my energy for when things got tight and they saw through my scheme. Then I'd be running full steam. Running would certainly feel good, but I have to say that the small of my back felt vulnerable.

A few yards before I reached the stuck arrow, I heard yelling and hollering. I chanced a quick look over my shoulder and saw the runners had already started. Scar, I assumed, was in the lead—so much for fair play. I snatched the arrow up and swung it over my head as I ran, picking up the pace a little, hoping I was far enough away so they wouldn't notice my leg was fine. I was going to throw it away but shoved it into my waistband instead. It wasn't much of a weapon, but it would be better than nothing. After another twenty yards, I looked over my shoulder and saw the runners were gaining on me.

I picked up my pace again as I started up the long slope. I wasn't worried about masking my trail yet, since they could still see me. If I lived, that would come later when I was in country less familiar to these braves. All I wanted now was to get away. After I'd been running for fifteen minutes, I started passing clumps of aspen with new leaves shooting out. I dodged in and about the trees, and the runners were out of sight although not far behind. I was working my legs like the shaft on a spinning loom, taking long strides as I burned up the hillside. My breathing was deep and regular, so I could have talked to someone had they been beside me. My arms and legs were moving together in a good rhythm. The sweat fell freely from my face and chest. The light breeze coming toward me from the top of the slope was refreshing and welcome.

By a copse of aspen trees, I noticed the dead fall looked like it had just been ripped apart. A bear, probably a grizzly, had gone on the rampage very recently, tearing up logs looking for grubs. I gave a mighty wide circle about the group of trees. I didn't want to get bogged down by deadfall with bare feet, nor did I want to stumble into an angry animal. Running into grizzly when you don't expect it is a major problem in this country. At the top of the ridge, the land flattened out into a plateau, forming another slope that wound into the foothills. Instead of running up the spine, I took a sharp right on the hard ground and dropped over the edge into a pocket of large quaking aspen. I quickly worked my way between the trees and down the steep bank until I was breaking through tangles of buck brush and choke cherry. I didn't bother to work around anything but the thickest stuff. I plowed into the snarled growth like a man chopping hay in bottomland. I could feel the branches slap my face and bite my skin, but I kept running, glad to be alive, knowing I had to keep my lead.

As I reached the bottom, my throat was starting to dry and swells of misgiving boiled up in my stomach as I pressed through. Was this the right choice? Should I have run farther up the ridge? I kicked such thoughts out and moved on. I'd flushed out pockets of mule deer with fawns. Such slopes were favorite feeding areas. Deer loved scrub brush. Once, to my left, I saw a small herd of elk, skirting me as I charged on. At the bottom of the canyon, a small stream bubbled over mossy rocks and fallen logs. I stopped and knelt by the pool. I drank slowly, careful not to take in too much. I shoved my head under the water and held it there.

Most men run down hill when they're chased. It's the easiest way to get distance. The Crows would likely assume I'd keep running down this canyon. I plunged into the stream for fifty yards making obvious, clumsy signs as I went down hill. I went another hundred yards, making only a few tracks. After another twenty yards, I made a less obvious sign by the side of the creek, but I knew the Crow would find it. My tracks were pointing downhill.

Then while standing on smooth rock, I dried off my feet and carefully made my way up the rocky bank on large boulders up the canyon. At all times I was careful not to step on the mossy sides or dislodge any dirt. I pushed back up the draw. I wouldn't fool them for long, but I might buy an extra fifteen minutes. They'd lose my sign and have to retrace my trail. They could do it, but it would take some scouting.

The further up the canyon I went, the more it started to narrow. I couldn't take time to hide my trail any longer, so I dropped down to the stream where I could move more quickly. I was cautious about where I stepped, placing my feet only on rocks or smooth logs. I was as careful as I could be under the circumstances. With difficulty, I worked up a narrow watercourse that fed into the main stream, walking on the hard stuff whenever I could. Maybe they might follow up the main stream for a few minutes before back tracking. Moving up the feeder canyon was getting difficult. The bed was strewn with boulders and fallen logs, making for slow going, and the sides were steep. I followed the route for several hundred yards until I came to a pinnacle about thirty feet high, a pool of water at its base.

I took a long drink as I pondered my next move.

Without waiting to work out the details, I started up the side of the canyon through the pines. The going was thick and slow. Running was out of the question, so was a fast walk. All I could say was I was moving forward at a steady stride. The deadfall was hard on my bare feet as I worked over the maze of fallen logs. I tore them up. After a quarter of a mile, I was finally at the top of the ridge. I could see the peaks of the Wind Rivers to my right and open slopes and parks.

I took off across the ridge at a good, steady trot. After going for a spell, I turned to check my back trail. Against the horizon, closer than I'd hoped, were two runners, and they weren't far behind.

CHAPTER 8

I knew I couldn't shake them for long, but I needed to give myself breathing space.

It's hard to think about what a body ought to do when he has folks on his back trail. Each decision is critical. I came to a flat point on the ridge, so I threw another look over my shoulder. About a half mile back, or so I guessed, were the two fastest runners, sticking to my trail like bloodhounds after a coon. Another brave was breaking out of the tangled deadfall at the top of the steep canyon. The other two must be farther back. They'd worked out my trail too quickly! Yet I was glad to see them strung out. The more they were stretched out, the better for me.

I had a decision to make and I had to make it fast. The ridge I was on was dividing into three possible routes. I could keep going north, the way I'd been running, since it looked like this ridge might keep going for miles. I could head off west along a shorter ridge that branched off and up into the heart of the Wind Rivers. Or I could drop off southwest into a valley that had just opened below me. It was my life I was playing with and I didn't want to make a mistake. Least of all, I didn't want to get myself boxed in. I had to take a track that would get me away from these braves. I had to try and lose them sooner or later if I could get far enough ahead.

Without another thought, I dropped over the lip of the steep canyon, moving around large boulders and such, making my way down into the valley. I liked the way it looked. It was a couple of miles wide and at least eight or nine miles long. There was a dark green river running through the middle, and the valley was mostly open once you got away from the water. Here and there along the stream were oxen-sized clumps of willow brush and choke cherry bushes clogging the edges. Every now and then, in the bends of the river, were big green groves of cottonwoods.

The willows and brush were actually a comfort to me. If something went wrong and the braves got too close, I could hide like a rabbit and lose myself in the snarled thickets. Some of those willow stands were a hundred yards deep. It took some time to get down the slope. It was steep and rocky. I went carefully so as not to take a fall in my eagerness. Once I made the valley floor, I could see those first two braves starting over the edge up on the rim. I took off with some speed when I saw them. I passed a group of large cottonwoods near the river and enjoyed the grass on my bare feet. I knew they could see me, so I made no attempt to hide where I was going. I was making a beeline directly away. I knew I'd stick out like a Quaker at a poker table. My plan now was distance. I wanted to put steps between us. I figured it would be about a half hour before the rest of the Crows started down the slope. When we were all on the flat, I could start to be a little tricky about my trail.

I found a buffalo path running even with the river. The ground was soft, but not too muddy, so I could make good time. My running came easy, but it does when you're running for your life. The thought of a lance through your chest is good motivation. Over the years, the trail had been worn smooth by the big beasts. I was getting a mite hungry, but I pushed the pains in the pit of my stomach out of my mind, concentrating instead on a fluid running motion, my legs stretching out to eat up the trail, arms swinging in stride to keep a good balance. In a couple of places, the ground turned muddy and I had to slow down some because it was hard to pull my feet out of the ooze. It actually helped me pace myself so I didn't get overly weary.

For almost an hour, I ran up the trail at a good clip without being careless. I was starting to feel it some and my chest began to burn and my side ached like I'd been gut-shot. I slowed to half a run and the pains went away. My hair was wet and my back and chest were soaked with sweat. When I took deep breaths, I could smell sweat, the musty scent of turned up mud and new grass mingled with a hint of cottonwood. Occasionally I'd run by growths of wild roses. For long stretches, it was grassy all the way to the riverbank. Sometimes the trail would take me past clumps of willow mixed with thick batches of wild choke cherry and buck brush. In such places, my worst fear, besides the braves coming up on my tail, was running into a silvertip feeding on new grasses or baby willow shoots. In early spring, grizzlies flocked into such places to eat plants. They're somewhat cranky, not being long out of their winter dens. They're spiteful and hateful if you cross them. Not only are they cantankerous, they'll run you down for exercise and swat off your head for fun. They don't take to intruders by nature, but in the spring they're more likely than other times to come at you, especially if it's a she bear with young.

Most folks don't know it, but big bears, besides Indians and the cold, killed a whole lot of the early mountain men, especially in the days when they carried Kentucky long rifles that shot a pea-sized chunk of lead. From what I hear, it made a bear madder than ever after you shot him without doing any damage. The bear would then charge over to gnaw on you and bend up your shooting iron. The Hawken has a lot more power. It shoots a piece of lead about the size of your thumb. But even with it, no man with half his wits wanted to stand down a griz charge with only one rifle. These bears are mean and soak up a lot of lead before they give up their ghost. A man, running like I was, just naturally makes a half-mad bear want to charge anyway. Your running is like calling it out. When you're close to a bear, it's best to back up gracefully or climb a tree. Running is like a dinner bell telling a bear to come and get you.

If I turned a corner and found myself close to a bear, the chances were better than even he'd come out for me because I was moving. I'd be threatening to him and he wouldn't take it lightly. I'd come across several sets of fresh tracks on this buffalo path, all made within the last few hours. I'd bet the farm those bears were only a few hundred yards off this trail in those thickets, stuffing themselves on willows and plants. Under normal circumstances, I'd never travel this close to a riverside thicket this time of the year. I'd have made my way out in the open where I could keep an eye on the thick stuff, staying a healthy distance from the bank.

I was more worried about Crows than silvertips, so I kept running down the buffalo path, my eyes scanning for bear, much more frightened of what was coming up the mouth of this pretty little valley. When the trail came near the water, I stopped and took a drink. The river was ice cold from snowmelt. I didn't take in much, just a few sips at a time, then a few more. I was losing a lot of water, sweating it off, and I dearly wanted to drink a bucket full, but I knew better. A lot of quick drinks would take me farther than one long one. I wasn't satisfied, but I kept going.

I surely couldn't take on a handful of braves at once, but if I could get them stretched out and divided, the odds would be more in my favor. The day was passing quickly and that had me fretting. I ran for another ten minutes at a good pace, then slowed down to a trot. It was time for action. I wasn't sure what I was going to do, but I kept my eyes open. By now I thought I should be almost halfway through the valley, maybe more. After ten minutes, I took a trail that branched off. I took it and as I expected, it was a spur heading indirectly for the river. It was getting late in the day. The trail wandered a quarter mile in and out of willow and choke cherry tangles before it led directly to the bank. I startled a moose and her calf. Several times the trail took me through clusters of cottonwoods. I jumped over the deadwood at one point and narrowly avoided a sharp branch that would have ripped my right foot wide open.

The trail went directly into the water, and I could see where it picked up again on the other side. I plunged into the icy current. The river was mostly waist deep but easy to cross otherwise, except for one stretch where the rocks were slippery and I nearly lost my footing. When I got to the opposite bank, I stepped out and began walking. I looked about, taking special note of my surroundings. It cost me time, time I hoped I had, but I walked up the stream for more than a hundred yards, making my sign obvious, weaving up on the bank and down into the water. I walked back to where I'd crossed. Next, I walked downstream a few hundred yards and did the same thing, making my sign as noticeable as I could.

Then I took off up the path. The earth was muddy near the water and I made deep prints. I started trotting up the trail. At some gopher holes, I stopped and filled my pockets and fists with dirt. I kicked about the holes, as if I'd stood there and shuffled without thinking. As the ground got harder, I started to leave less sign. By the time I was a quarter of a mile from the crossing, I was using all the woodcraft I could to mask my passing. At times I'd take some of the dirt in my pocket and sift it carefully over where I'd stepped, or I'd stoop over, while standing on a rock, and blow on the ground so it would look untracked. The trail led higher, sloping up as it left the valley. The ground was hard and rocky. At the top of a small rise, I stepped only on stones for several hundred yards. If I had to touch the ground with my feet, I made sure they left no mark or I masked the sign as best I could. I was picking my way back toward the river, angling toward a big clump of willow and choke cherry.

My hope was to make that thicket before they came to the crossing and caught me in the open. It was slow work when you're trying to step so no one can follow you. The rocks were fewer as I neared the river, but by twisting about I managed to make it almost to the willows without making many noticeable marks. Now that doesn't mean a tracker can't follow you. He can. It just means it's not going to be easy for him and it's going to take a while to work out your trail.

One of the reasons I'd shifted directions so often was so they'd not be able to second guess where I was heading. They'd all have to stay on my trail, instead of leaving two to follow my sign while the other three tried to head me off. I hoped this would work. You can't make a lot of mistakes. With a little luck, I hoped they'd keep running up the trail for another mile or so. They'd think I was still on the trail if they didn't cut my sign on the hard ground. My plan was that, by moving up and down the river, I'd give them the idea that I wasn't sure what to do or where to go. When I finally decided to take up the trail, it would make them think I was determined to go the course for a while in that direction.

Maybe they'd get careless and it would be nearly dark or the next morning before they got back onto my real sign. The edges of the willows were thick and about five feet tall where I was facing them. I was as close as I could get without making sign, standing on a fallen log. The ground about me was wet, and there wasn't a handy rock in sight to step on. If the Crow guessed I'd headed for the willows, they'd search along the edges for my entry. They'd see where I stepped—either by the broken or bent branches or by my tracks in the soft earth.

Since the log was only few feet from the edge of the brush, I backed up to get a running start. At the edge, I jumped for all I was worth like an old bullfrog with something to prove. I flung myself head first into the thicket. I figured I was at least four feet from the edge when I landed on my shoulder, suspended by some thorny brush. They'd not easily tell where I entered unless they were inside the thicket themselves. Making no effort to conceal my movement from here on, I worked toward the riverbank. I needed distance, and I had to start shaking them off my trail. The willows came right to the edge of the bank. The only way you could walk the bank at this spot would be to get your feet wet or fight the brush. I hoped they'd do neither, but I wouldn't have bet on it.

I'd no sooner looked upstream at where I'd started than two Crow Indians stepped onto the sandy bank and carefully looked over the area. I'd made it with no time to spare. I looked upstream again, but I didn't look directly at them. Some men in the wild have a sixth sense about being stared at. I was a third of a mile, if that, from where I'd crossed earlier. I prayed my false trail would fool them for a spell. Both braves stopped and took a drink and seemed to be talking to each other. I looked down at my feet for some reason. When I looked up, there was a third brave.

A warrior was removing his leggings and loincloth. Carrying a bundle over his head in one hand, his weapons in another, he crossed the stream. He set the bundle of clothes down and, taking just his spear, he started following my sign downstream. Bending over to feel my tracks with his finger, he searched the banks. When he stopped to turn back, he was less than two hundred yards away. It was probably my imagination, but he seemed to look directly at my hiding place in the bushes. He stood for at least five minutes looking and listening. Buck naked with only a spear, following sign as naturally as he did, he seemed more animal than man.

He suddenly turned and followed my back trail with little interest up to where he started. I felt a cold shiver running down my spine, barely daring to breathe for fear of giving away my hiding place. The brave was Scar. The slowest runners had arrived and they all crossed the river and got on the far side. Two men scouted my tracks upstream and one was following my trail on the buffalo path. The last two put on their clothing and started off after him at a trot. As soon as they were out of sight, I leaped into the icy river and walked upstream in the mud for several hundred yards. The water over the mud on the edges of the river was calm. It would take almost a day before my tracks would be covered by stream silt. I wanted them obvious but not too obvious. I stopped where Scar had paused to study my tracks. I got out of the stream and walked over to where he'd stood. I deliberately put my footprint over his track and drew a small cross in several of his prints. I wanted him to now think twice about me. I went back upstream, walking for another fifty yards before working my way into the middle.

In the strong current where they couldn't see my tracks, I tucked my knees up and let the heavy drift carry me downstream. I hoped my plan to cover my trail would buy more time. Moving upstream might put them off for a moment. They'd worked out my back trail sooner or later. When they came to the river bank, they couldn't be sure if I'd gone up or downstream—even though my tracks were indicating I was going up. The sign would be clear for several hundred yards, then disappear. They'd have to divide to search out my escape path. They also would have to examine the banks among the thick brush for where I got out.

The first side of the river I'd been on was covered with growth, some of it very thick. This would slow the search down. The only way to work out my trail was to divide up until one of them cut sign. The sun was starting to go down and, with any luck, they wouldn't make it back to the river before it was almost dark. That would mean they'd have to wait until the morning to take up the chase, after they found my trail again.

I'd keep floating as long as I could stand the cold, which seemed as icy as January. Because the river twisted, it would take a long time to float far, but at least I wouldn't be leaving sign. I'd hoped to stay in the stream as long as I could, but the water was bone chilling. I'd floated around two meandering curves and was about to make for the bank while I could still move when the water became shallow. In the shoals, a drifting log that must have fallen in a windstorm was caught on a jagged rock. In the knee-deep water, I freed the tree. As the current got deeper, I was able to climb on and stay mostly above the water. I floated for several miles, occasionally getting caught in the riffles, but I could not stand the cold any longer.

I clumsily made my way toward a grove of cottonwood trees, trembling across the rocks, avoiding the soft spots where I might make a track. In the shallow water, I took off my pants and wrung them out several times. I stood on a rock until my skin had dried so I wouldn't drip on the soft soil. It might be spotted by a sharp eye. Holding my wet pants, my belt, and the arrow, I surveyed the landscape. I had to find a place to get warm.

The cold water sapped my strength and the chilly evening was worrying me. It might be below freezing soon, and I had to think about the coming night. The sun had just dropped under the horizon and within a half hour it would be too dark to see. Shivers ran down my body and my toes felt numb. I had to find shelter for the night and I had to do it right away or I would freeze to death. The problem was I had no way of making a fire. When I looked up, the sky was pale across the saw-toothed peaks. Silvery shadows started to creep up everywhere. A thin moon had slipped up over a peak while a faint breeze rustled the new leaves in the top of the grove. I had two choices: I could run for the rest of the night so I'd stay warm, or I could find some sort of shelter. The problem with running was there wasn't a lot of light to see by. If I knew where I was going, it might be a different story, but it would be tough to see how to step on the trail. Then once I got out of the valley, which wouldn't take that long if a man was going to move all night, I'd have to decide on a direction and that would be difficult in low light. If I got in rough country or had a stroke of bad luck and stepped in a hole, I'd likely break my leg.

My only comfort was I knew the braves, wherever they were now, could not follow me after dark. I was getting cold, very cold.

I didn't worry about covering up my trail. I made my way into the cottonwood grove to get out of the breeze. There were a number of dead falls and a lot of dry leaves from last fall. It hadn't rained for a few days, so maybe they would be dry enough to make a bed and I could bury myself in them. Sandwiched between two logs, I'd slept in leaves more than once. Of course I'd had clothes on and wasn't chilled to begin with.

With awkward hands, I started to scoop leaves when I noticed a giant cottonwood lying on the ground. The core had been rotten so it had weakened and fallen. Once on the ground, insects had eaten out much of the insides. Breaking the pithy center, I was able to enlarge the cavity enough so I could squeeze my naked body into it. Then, I crawled in feet first. Using my toes, I broke away more of the center. I also plugged up a few holes so the cold air could not come in and so my body heat could be trapped. I stuffed in leaves I'd gathered so there wasn't much air about my feet and legs. I pushed my way down into the rotten tree until my head was a foot in from the opening. I pulled in all the leaves I could reach and blocked the hole near my head by working loose wood and sawdust into place.

It was chilly, but my body heat soon warmed the cocoon up so I was comfortable. My feet were cut up and they hurt, but they weren't as bad as you might think. Wearing moccasins, like I usually did, makes feet tougher than wearing boots. The soaking my feet had taken in the river while I was floating had done them good, getting all the thorns and such out and opening up the cuts so they would drain and get cleaned. The crunching of the leaves as I settled in was comforting and pleasant. You hear stories of folks sleeping in hollowed out trees and you wonder how much of it is talk and how much is real. I can tell you, it's not bad.

For the first time all day, my legs started to ache and I felt some muscle cramps. I was mighty tired, too tired to think much about food, even if my stomach was growling.

I lay back on my rolled-up pants, shut my eyes, and let sleep start to take me. Tomorrow would have to be worried about later. Nothing would be moving in the dark and I needed sleep. Waves of warmth surged through my legs and chest as I drifted off. I listened to the sound of the water a few feet away.

Chapter 9

A twig snapped and I awoke with a start.

It was past dawn and something was moving nearby. Several shafts of light streaked through a crack on the top of my sleeping log. I was mad at myself for sleeping so hard, something a man in my position had no business doing. If I wasn't careful, I'd lose my lead, or worse, find myself trapped like a fox in a henhouse. I dared not move for fear of rustling the leaves that had kept me warm. I held my breath and listened, hoping my shelter wouldn't become a coffin. I'd slept deep, too deep. I'd planned to be on the trail at sunup.

For the moment, at least, I was trapped and would die where I lay as soon as that warrior figured out exactly where I was. It wouldn't take long, either, once he found where I'd left the river and that I'd crawled into this hollow log. I clutched the arrow in my right hand, and it gave me some comfort, but I wished it was that

.52 caliber pistol. I tried to see through a small knot in the side of the trunk. I moved my head slowly, not making a sound, putting my left eye against the opening, straining to see the outside. He was getting closer, not worrying about how loud he was, toying with me to see if I'd bolt.

My stomach cinched up like a too-tight saddle. I pondered my options, wondering if I should try to come out, arrow and pants in hand, and try to make a run for it. I'd be risking a shaft or a lance in my back. Or should I wait here and take a chance on having him blade me where I lay? I was helpless. I knew I could die here and now. How fast could I come out of this cottonwood tree coffin? Like my life depended upon it, likely. But would that be fast enough? The steps were heading my way.

I heard another twig snap and then I saw him. The brave stalking me had dark brown, stilt-like legs with hooves. Then I saw her long nose. A yearling cow moose had wandered in the copse of trees and was munching spring grass and scratching her head on anything handy, which at this point happened to be the fallen tree I was lodging in. I'd had enough. I pushed out the leaves and the pith I'd used to plug up the end of the tree and wormed my way into the brisk morning. For a second, the young moose looked with uncertainty as a large white, bare-naked object struggled out of the core of that tree. With a jerk of her head, she bolted upstream into the clearing to eat the budding spring flowers. The cow looked back to check on me cautious-like then began to chew on her breakfast.

It hurt to stand on my cut up feet. I slipped into my damp pants and started limping up the trail. After twenty minutes of walking, I figured out how to ignore some of the throbbing. What ached worse than my feet was the gnawing in my belly. I was under no illusion. I knew they'd be on my trail soon enough and I had to make tracks. I was cursing my late start. After a few more minutes, I stopped and took a long drink in the icy water. Somewhat refreshed, I broke into a slow trot, as much to warm up as to distance myself from where I'd camped. There was no time to worry about masking my back tracks—all I wanted was to get as far from where I'd slept as I could. I trotted up a gentle slope near the canyon side of the river. The grass made good running. It was still cold in the shade since it was a little frosty. Yellow and white flowers were busting out in all their glory. Bees were busy going to and fro, seeming not to have a care in the world. There wasn't much cover out in the open where I was, so I felt vulnerable. I picked up my pace some, moving up the ridge at a slow run, trying to get to the top of the canyon before I was spotted by Crow eyes that might happen to be looking this way.

Coming up this long ridge, I'd be very easy to spot. Running didn't come as easy today as it had yesterday, but I kept going anyway. It was mind over body, a body that kept saying no. I needed food, and my feet and muscles hurt. I have to say, however, I sure liked those flowers and wanted to keep appreciating them for years to come. Spring is pretty anytime, even when you're being chased and the growling in your stomach could be heard ten feet to the side. Makes you want to see a lot more springs and eat a lot more breakfasts.

I eased over the top of the rise, bent low, almost crawling to keep from being sky-lined. I dropped down to check my back trail. Sure enough, I was being followed. He came out of the thick stuff and was about to walk into the trees where I'd camped in that tree. My trail would be obvious. I was sure he hadn't seen me come up the slope since he was looking down. He wasn't looking off in the distance. I watched him for a few moments. He was alone and I was glad of that. I kept an eye on him until he picked up my trail and started after me. If he'd been smart, he'd have gone back and gotten the others, but knowing a little about Crows like I did, it was my guess he wanted me for himself. He'd found my sign and he'd want the honor of taking me out alone. In the Crow's world, there was amusement but little honor in a group kill.

Well that was just what he was going to get . . . me alone! I'd see to that!

Looking at him made me madder by the minute. Besides, I was hungry and my feet hurt. I'd lost my furs, my rifles, my horses, my knife, and my good humor. It was time to even up the score. I realize this was pretty bold thinking for a bare-footed man who had a single arrow and nothing else to fight with. But I didn't care. I observed him a few minutes more to make double sure he didn't turn and go for the others. When he started up the slope, I took off at a dead run, forgetting my feet and my hunger. He'd have me alone all right, but he'd have me on my terms. I needed some distance first and I needed some time to make a plan. I paced myself after a fast half-mile sprint and kept going at a good trot for well over an hour.

I ran through several gullies and clumps of leafing aspen. I was twisting, but leaving a good, clear track for him to follow. I wanted my sign to come easy so he wouldn't have to work to follow me. At the right spot, I turned into a bunch of willows and choke cherry brush and started back to a place I'd made a mental note of. My trail had gone through a gully near a group of pines and several large boulders. It was a perfect place for a trap. I would wait for him like a mountain cat waits for a mule deer and even the score. With my arrow in one hand and a fist-sized rock in the other, I crouched behind a small boulder and several clumps of sagebrush.

I didn't have to wait long. He'd made time, moving at a good trot, following my sign with a glance here and there. It was Dull Horn, one of the braves who'd brought me in. He had a lance in his left hand, a bow strapped in the otter quiver on his back. He was the best tracker among them. How I wished I'd my knife instead of a granite rock.

I could see him trotting through the grass and trees. I avoided eye contact since it might give me away. He came past the crooked pine and was just beneath the boulder. It had to be a surprise, especially with him carrying that lance. I had one chance and I had to do it right the first time.

About the time he was even with me, I sprung my trap. I was in the air and nearly on him, swinging that rock, trying to make a dent in his head before he could get his war lance up. Out of the corner of his eye, he saw me and turned as I was almost upon him. He moved slightly to the side, bringing his free arm up to shield his face. It was too late to adjust my swing. His unstrung bow deflected my arm a mite and my rock glanced off the side of his buffalo horn headdress. It stunned him though. He dropped his lance, but it didn't check him as much as I'd wanted. He turned to face me, reaching for a blade in a sheath hanging about his neck.

I had to stop him! And fast.

A rock is a fine weapon, but it's no match for a knife. The rock was in my right hand at my side, but the arrow in my left was at chest level. Using it as a knife, I thrust it down with all my strength, trying to spear his knife hand before he could lunge at my belly. I missed his hand by a Mississippi mile, but I buried the shaft deep into his thigh. He forgot about me and his knife and looked down at the blood soaking into his leggings and at the shaft that was buried into six inches of flesh.

When he paused, I brained him with the granite chunk. He crumbled to the ground as if he were dead. I had nothing against him, but he would have done me in if given the opportunity. I felt no malice. I took his weapons. He had a fine lance and a very fine bow made from the horn of mountain sheep. His knife was inferior to my own, but it was cared for and moderately sharp. Next, I undid his moccasins. I know what you're thinking. I should have grabbed his gear and made some tracks. I'll tell you, I just couldn't do it. Leaving him would mean he'd die. If I helped him, he'd live. I had to help him—it's the way my folks brought me up.

From a nearby spruce, I quickly collected some gobs of pitch and rubbed it on my feet to stop the bleeding. Then I slipped his moccasins on and they fit, but were a little tight. They were freshly made from smoked moose hide. I stripped off Dull Horn's shirt and put it on. It was a little small so I slipped the point of his knife under the arms and loosened up the seams so I could move freely. I relieved him of his possibles bag, which had an extra string for his bow, jerky, a pouch of tinder, flint and steel, pemmican, and his medicine sack.

I'd hit him pretty hard, but he was breathing good. I pulled him near the water, about fifty feet off the trail, to a place that would have full sun all day. I sat him up against an old pine snag and used some willow leaves to help stop the bleeding. He had quite a knot where I'd rocked him. The arrow in his leg kept the bleeding down, but it would eventually have to come out. Then he would bleed like a stuck pig. Cutting around the shaft carefully, I pulled off his left legging. Then I removed the other so I could make another pair of moccasins on the trail later, if need be, or I could wear them if the weather got cold.

Using dry wood, I quickly kindled a small fire that would burn hot and smokeless. When the fire was going, I put the tip of his blade in the hottest part. I stuffed some of his buffalo jerky in my mouth. I wanted to wolf it right down but I forced myself to work it slowly in my jaws. I could feel it give me strength. I must have been really hungry since I thought it was the best tasting dried meat I'd ever had, even better than my own. Grabbing his lance, I climbed a rise that overlooked the river basin to see if anyone was onto my sign yet. I dared not stay long, just long enough to get this man stable and I'd be moving out. I watched the trail and hill for a few minutes, but didn't see any movement.

By the time I got back to the fire, the blade was red hot. Dull Horn was mumbling something but he hadn't moved. He was still out cold, but the bleeding on his head had stopped. Using his buffalo head piece, I gathered water and bathed his temple, cleaning his head wound before I bound it up with a piece of leather from his loincloth. With his head taken care of, I went to work on his leg. I always heard pulling an arrowhead out the way it came in, especially one buried this far, would do more damage than pushing it through. It hadn't cut any arteries, at least I didn't think it had, so he had a good chance of being okay if I got the wound taken care of, the arrow out, and the bleeding stopped. I got a strong hold on the shaft, and shoved it the rest of the way through his leg.

I'd never done this before, but I'd seen it done once. It's not pleasant, but in the mountains you have to do what has to be done. I wasn't about to let this man die if I could help him. His wound was bleeding mighty hard which, to a point, was a good thing since it might keep the poison out. Next, I took that hot knife blade, the tip burning orange, and laid it across the top of the wound, searing it shut. Then I laid it over the bottom part and seared it shut. Burnt flesh has a smell of its own, but there weren't a lot of choices. I packed both sides of his leg with some willow leaves, which are supposed to be good on burns, then bound it with loosely with strips of leather. There wasn't much more I could do but leave him. I thanked him for his possibles and weapons. I was starting to think I might have a chance.

I put the butt end of a log in the fire with a few more twigs to get it started good. I sat his pemmican and medicine pouch on the ground beside him and took off at a fast run. A small piece of jerky was flavoring my mouth. I'd shoved his knife and sheath into my waistband since a knife about your neck is an annoyance and around my neck I couldn't get it fast. His lance felt good in my hand. I adjusted my grip on the shaft as I ran, moving out at a healthy pace. I guessed I was running about five or six miles an hour. Having something on my feet made a difference. The unstrung bow in the other quiver thumped on my back in a nice sort of way, helping me keep pace.

I'd made my share of bows, but Dull Horn had a fancy one and I admired it. I was pleased to be the new owner. Most bows in this part of the world were made out of Osage orange, juniper, ash, cedar, or oak cut in the winter to prevent cracking. A horn bow was a valued weapon—the horns of mountain sheep being the most coveted. This was the sort of bow a serious hunter would use. I doubt a warrior would take this weapon into battle.

Making a horn bow is a good four-month job, taking a lot of careful labor. Not just anyone could do it. The Indian has to be a master craftsman. The bowmaker skillfully cuts off slices of horn, then glues and wraps them together carefully. After that, it's shaped and crafted some more. It's glued again and filed and glued and filed until it's the right size, which is about four feet. I'm told that bows used to be a lot longer before the Plains Indians started to hunt on horses. Since that time, the size of the bows became smaller because they could get closer to what they were aiming at, and it's easier to shoot with a short bow at a running gallop.

It was tradition that the back of horn bows be covered by the skin of a rattlesnake since it brought good luck. This bow was no exception. Few things are prettier than a fine horn bow—unless it's a wink and a smile from a mountain girl at a square dance. I was glad it was mine. Dull Horn would have more than a sore head when he realized I'd taken his prized weapon, along with a dozen of his crafted arrows. Maybe he needed to stick with weapon-making. I'm not sure he was cut out to be a warrior, although he was still young.

I hoped he fared well. It might take two braves off my trail. He was in no shape to come after me, and he'd have to have help to get back to camp. He wasn't going to be moving very fast with a bad leg and a throbbing skull. He had water if he needed it. And he could add wood from the snag, building up the fire, without moving if he wasn't found by night. There was nothing more I could do.

It felt good to be running. I could have eaten about twenty Mormon flapjacks and ten pounds of side meat, but at least the jerky was keeping me going and I was sparing with it. I had a good lead, and I could make a fire in the night to keep warm if I needed to since I had the makings. I had something on my feet, and most of all it felt good to have weapons. The day was warm and the new growth was pleasant for the eye.

As I was rounding a steep bank in the small basin, a foul stench in the air almost burned my eyes. I knew what it was, but it didn't register until it was too late. I heard an angry bellow and the old boar indignantly drew his head out of the butt end of a rotting elk carcass and glared at me, the intruder who threatened his meal. Rearing on his hind legs to get a better look, he coughed and spat. After dropping to all fours, he woofed like an infuriated dog, then started snapping his jaws together with such force you could have heard it across the river.

I didn't stop to think. Instead, I jumped up for the branches on the nearest aspen, dropping that lance, pulling myself up. I don't imagine I'd ever climbed a tree as fast as I climbed that one. I was seven or eight feet high when it charged. I wasn't up as high as I wanted to be when that griz rushed, but I was climbing. He rammed my tree like a mad bull. The force nearly knocked me to the ground and seemed to loosen up the aspen's roots. I wasn't sure it was going to hold.

Scrambling higher, I watched him paw the trunk with mighty strikes, like a boxer, raking off fist fulls of bark with each punch. He had half a mind to beat that tree down and I think he could have done it had he kept trying. Aspen aren't plugged into mother earth that deep—a powerful grizzly or a good north wind has been known to tumble even a big one. For about five minutes, he circled like he was guarding me, knowing I was there, not knowing how to get me down. He stared up with his pale pig-like eyes and got madder. I'd found myself a good perch, hooking my legs about the trunk of the tree in case he made another sudden charge for the trunk.

I slipped off my bow and strung it. Then I knocked an arrow and waited. The silvertip stood on his two hind feet, a terrifying sight. He was over ten feet tall and capable of killing a buffalo with one smash of his powerful paw. When he turned to stare directly at me, I aimed to the left of a cream colored patch in the middle of his muscular chest. I anchored the arrow back to my jaw and let her fly. Instead of hitting him in the lungs where I'd aimed, I'd sunk that arrow high up on his chest right under his throat.

He clamored and bellowed and wheeled about three times grabbing for the shaft. I fired another and missed because he was moving. My third managed to sink into his lung behind his right front leg. He turned, spitting and biting at the new arrow in his side. He dug at the shaft, looking up at me. He made an awful howl, rushing headlong into that aspen again. I could feel the roots give a little. He grabbed at his chest again and bit into the lance I'd left at the foot of the tree, shaking it like a dog would a rat. He moved as if something might relieve the pain or at least even up the score for the sharp objects that had invaded his body. He broke the fletching of the arrow in his lungs when he rolled over.

His side and chest were bloody and he was going to die sooner or later, but dying wouldn't come easily for an animal this determined to live.

From where I sat, there was nothing I could do to speed it up. There was enough fight left in him to send a band of men to Saint Peter's Gate and I dared not leave my perch. I had more arrows left, but I didn't want to waste them since I might need them for other targets. I made a note to take some practice with Dull Horn's bow since I seemed to hit right of where I aimed. Of course, sitting in a tree, shooting almost straight down at a mad bear that wants to rip your head off is not the best way to test a new weapon.

After fifteen minutes his sides were heaving up and down, blood matted on his long, grizzled fur—his silver cinnamon coat stained a dark crimson. Light red foam was frothing from his mouth, a sure sign of a lung wound. I watched him with sympathy. I always liked bears, even those who wanted to make me their lunch. There's something about a grizzly that puts a man in his place. Grizzly, like the wolf, are symbols of the wilderness. They represent a way of life and a freedom I deeply loved. And like the Indian and the mountain man, the grizzly, and the wolf for that matter, will pass into memory when civilization starts laying her ugly hand across a land that does not need saving. Wolves and grizzly are all that is good and wild and I hope I never see the day or walk the land when they aren't about.

In some creatures, there's just no defeat and you have to respect them for it. They don't know when to quit and they die before they compromise. The old boar let out a last shrill bellow and his sides stopped moving. He wasn't the first grizzly I'd taken, but he was the best and the most savage and the only one I ever hoped to shoot with a bow. I waited for a few more minutes to see that nothing moved. Carefully, I crept down the tree and picked up the chewed lance.

The bear's eyes looked dull so I touched the right one with my lance to make sure. An animal can fake death, but not a touch to his eye. The grizzly was dead all right. I hated to waste the hide, especially when it was fresh and not rubbed out like this one. But skinning a grizzly, let alone carrying a green hide, was a lot of work. I took my knife and cut off the claws and put them with my possibles. I pulled out a back strap and wrapped it in my legging. I guess I had about twenty pounds of meat, meat that would taste good over my evening fire.

The last thing I did before taking off was make a foot-long cut under the ribs, making a hole large enough to get the bear's heart out. I took a few big sticks and drove them into the soft ground. I placed the grizzly's heart on the sticks as a sign to those following me that I was a warrior who killed grizzly and feared nothing.

I centered it on the sticks, but not before I'd taken a big bite!

Chapter 10

It pained me to leave a perfectly good skin, but I needed to go now. I picked up my bear-chewed lance and started off at a fast trot, fingering the chewed part of the shaft as my legs stretched out to eat up some trail. I was hungry enough to eat a chuck wagon, but I didn't have time to stop and make a meal on this trail—not until dark that is.

Fighting Dull Horn and that feisty old silvertip had cost me traveling hours, time I could ill afford. A smart man had to assume they were on my trail. Wouldn't be too long before the other Crows, with Scar at the lead, unraveled my intentions and were coming down upon me like a pack of hounds on a cottontail. Seeing Dull Horn would only make them more resolved and angry.

With moccasins on, I could run longer and with less pain. The bottoms of my feet were still cut up but now they could start to heal. I soaked them when I could and dabbed the gashes and tears with pinesap. I put another piece of jerky in my mouth and started to work it around as I ran up the trail. When the sun was straight overhead, I came flat upon a she wolf and her cubs chasing mice in a grassy field—unaware until I nearly tripped over her. I gave them a start since it's not often you get that close to a wolf with cubs, even if the wind is in your face. It goes to show you, no matter how careful you are, a body can get snuck up on. The lesson wasn't lost on me.

I'd left the river valley and was crossing a grassy ridge. It was my plan to drop south into some deep gullies. The washes were steep so I had to slow down. Going fast in this stuff, a man could easily break or twist a leg. I slowed to a fast walk. At least it gave me time to catch my breath. I'd made no effort to mask my sign. I stuck mostly to game trails. I kept my eye on the sun so I would continue going south.

I passed a small herd of buffalo and a few cow elk with newly born calves. I was making good time for such broken country, crossing a number of gullies cut deep by the run off. Some were so steep I needed to slide down them. All the while, I couldn't help feeling something was not far down my back trail and closing in. You can't prove that kind of spooky feeling; it's something you just know and it haunts you. It's like you think someone is reading over your shoulder and you look up from your book and find you were right. Someone was gazing your way. Or you feel that someone is looking hard at you, so you look up from what you're doing and see someone is staring down at you without shame. Your eyes lock and a shudder starts down your back because you'd felt it before you actually knew it.

The hairs on the back of my neck were sticking up in a queer way, and I felt uncomfortable and restless. Every step I took was a step farther away, a step toward freedom. But someone or someones were close by, wanting a piece of my hide. Some call that feeling a sixth sense. Whatever it was, it was nagging me in a big way. I knew Scar was dogging my trail and he wouldn't give up.

Some scoff at a sixth sense, sometimes called a second sight, but I've come to believe it. Out in the wilderness, you might be planning to go up the right fork of some river. But when you get to it, a little voice tells you that even though it makes sense to go up that trail, something inside warns you to go the other way instead. So you follow that voice. You don't make fun of your feelings, instead you learn to follow them. Maybe you find out later that the right fork of the trail held some danger, maybe you never do. I've learned to live with my feelings and respect them.

I picked up the pace. The ground was hard and the trail I was on had petered out. Scar and his friends would have to start working a little bit harder. My only advantage was they didn't have an idea where I was heading. Of course, I wasn't so sure I knew myself. At least it wouldn't be easy for them to swing around and lay a stalk. I hadn't established a pattern yet and was liable to switch directions at any time.

I stepped into a steep draw making my way down an abrupt gully littered with rocks centuries of flash floods had left behind. I was able to jump across the boulders for nearly a quarter of a mile without making a track. Some were long leaps, but I never touched the ground. If a body were to look closely, he'd see I crushed or scraped some of the orange and yellow lichens that grew on the tops. But that was the only sign I'd left.

When I could go no farther, I scrambled my way up the bank climbing mostly on rocks. I put some more jerky in my mouth and started across the plateau. The sun was starting to hang long on the peaks and I was into patches of pine and aspen again. The going was a little rougher and I was making a steady climb. I figured that, since I'd fought the bear, I'd climbed several thousand feet. I stopped at a small creek and took a long drink. I was feeling my second day of running on only a few strips of jerky, but I dared not quit until it was dark. I was looking forward to a big piece of bear meat, but that would have to wait. There were at least three more hours before sundown.

Even though I was moving at a good pace, I put my buckskin shirt on. The late afternoon had a bite as soon as the sun dropped low or slid behind the peaks. It was going to be a cold night. Just before sundown, I slipped into the thick stuff. For fifteen minutes, I fought my way over deadfall. Pine bows caught me in the face when I wasn't looking. In the dim light I had to be careful about not walking into a sharp branch and losing an eye. Many times I got down on all fours and crawled beneath the thick overhead bows or underneath fallen logs. The trees weren't large, as far as pine trees go, but they were thick as hair.

No one would be able to find me in here after dark. I'd hear them coming a half mile away. Even when you're working at going quiet, you can sound like a bunch of blind buffalo stumbling. Several times I spooked does with their young.

I made camp at last light. Water had collected from the melt in a small depression from which I had a drink. Next to a fallen spruce log, I made my bed. I pushed up dry pine needles until they were about eight inches deep. I trimmed off a number of pine bows, weaving them together in a loose fashion for a makeshift blanket. Fuel wasn't a problem. You couldn't swing a dead barnyard cat without finding branches to burn.

With my knife, I cut out a section of sod eight inches deep, a foot wide, and as long as my arm. I gathered enough fuel to kindle my fire. Normally, it would be wise to make a fire and camp a mile or so away, but I hadn't dared stop before this. There was no moon, so it was dark as a cave, making it nearly impossible to move, let alone trail someone. What little light there was got closed out by the tops of the crowded stretch of pine trees. The trees were so thick you couldn't see my fire more than thirty feet off.

I carved off a thick steak and roasted it above the coals. While it was cooking, I started to weave a rack from pencil-sized willow so I could dry some bear meat during the night. I needed the meat. Besides, eating a good meal would reduce the weight I had to carry. I carved up most of the backstrap as thinly as I could in the firelight so it would dry quickly in the heat and smoke. I made a bed of pine bows and leaned back and had my dinner. When I was done, I had a long drink from a pool made by the melting snow. Ice was starting to form on the top.

I felt sleep coming after me. With a full belly, I slept sound, getting up a few times to bank the fire. Well before daybreak, I awoke with a start. It was cold and I was shivering. I stirred the coals and got my fire going. I cooked the steak I'd saved for breakfast. I kept the jerky on the rack. It was pretty dry, but I'd at least give it the benefit of my morning fire.

The sun still wasn't coloring up the day when I put out my fire and started moving. In fact, it was barely light enough to see. I covered the ashes with the sod I'd cut and carefully scattered my pine bow bed in the surrounding thickets. My preparations wouldn't stand a close look, but possibly a casual glance wouldn't reveal my camp.

My possibles bag was bulging with dried bear meat. I had a full stomach and a good night's rest. I crept through the forest, moving branches carefully, going around stuff I couldn't crawl through. I took in deep breaths of the morning pine, working my way a little higher but in the same direction as last evening. I hoped to come out a ways higher than where I'd entered. If my calculations were right, I'd keep going southwest and, sooner or later, hit the Green River.

I was making my way quiet as a cat. The air was still and chilly, so sound traveled a long ways. As the pines were starting to thin out, I thought I smelled just a hint of wood smoke and that wasn't good news. Careful as a mountain cat, I edged out of the thick stuff into clearings and aspen. A trace of smoke was hanging about the trees, but I couldn't tell where it was coming from since there was no breeze. If I moved too fast, my steps made little scraping sounds on the frost clinging to the grass.

After I'd gone a few hundred yards, I figured I knew where that fire was. The Crows had set up their camp close to where I'd drifted off into the thick pine forest. They had been losing light fast as the sun was dropping, so they had decided to camp and work my trail out in the morning. They'd been a lot closer than I'd known.

I started cutting a wide circle. If I was lucky, it would take an hour or more before they found where I'd spent the night and followed my trail out of the pine thicket to where I was now standing. I hoped, since I'd circled back the way I'd come, my actions would throw them off a little. You don't expect a man on the run to come back the way he came. Well, I should have cut a wide track about the smoke, but I didn't. The sun still hadn't started to color up the eastern horizon and they were loafing. Using all the cover nature gave me, I started coming in, coming in a very careful way. I was sure close. The breeze hadn't started up yet, and wouldn't for hours, so morning campfire smoke was still hanging in the tops of the pines and aspen. The camp was nearby. I got down and started crawling in. I could feel the frost on my fingertips and the hard-froze ground bit into my palms. I circled about patches of dirty snow, keeping on fallen pine needles as much as I could. I was mad enough to do something, but I wasn't stupid. I wasn't going to take them on at once. I'd strung up my bow and put a couple of arrows in my teeth. My war lance was in my left hand.

They'd made their camp next to an island of quakies by the base of a weather-twisted pine in the middle of a small meadow. When I worked my way to the edge of buck brush, I had a good view. Camp was a long stone's throw away. There they were, sitting about warming their hands. A couple of pieces of meat were roasting on embers. They'd likely taken some steaks from my bear, allowing them to keep moving since they wouldn't have to stop and hunt as they tracked me.

Good sense told me I ought to get out fast. But I couldn't, not now. One of them had my bear hide. Besides, I had a few extra arrows to burn. I was going to teach them a lesson from the book of Wolf Rockwell. Chapter one, verse one: get even with those who chase you with intent to scalp. I knew I was supposed to forgive all, at least that was what my friends the Mormons preached, but I wasn't feeling too Christian as I knocked one of the arrows onto my bow string. Mostly to be on the safe side, I waited to see how many there were. I wanted to know what I was up against. Scar was sitting next to the pine, eating and no doubt giving orders like the self-important man he was.

Looked like there were only two warriors after me. Odds were getting better and I was feeling confident, maybe too confident. For Crows, they weren't being careful about their camp. I suppose they didn't think that I was much of a threat. They were wrong! And I have to say I felt a little insulted that they judged me so poorly.

I must have moved or something looked out of place. A brave looked right where I was hiding for a couple of seconds. He turned in a casual sort of way, like nothing was wrong, took his bow up from the ground where it was sitting, and started stringing her up. He must have seen me in my hiding spot and was going to venture an arrow at me. He was hoping I hadn't noticed him looking at me. My horn bow was up to it. The arrows Dull Horn had crafted were artful. I'd killed a grizzly already and it made me feel sure and sassy. I was just over fifty yards, but I was sure I could make it. When that brave turned his back, pretending to be warming himself on the fire, I knew I had only an instant to decide if I was going to take the shot. He'd knocked an arrow and was drawing back his bow before turning.

A second before he whipped around to fire, I drew back that arrow, hugging my cheek comfortable-like. I anchored the string on my lip for half a second, controlling my excited breathing. Holding my breath a split second, I visualized that arrow flying straight and true for the middle of his Crow back. You never want to pluck a bowstring since it makes the arrow fly funny. So holding it just a hair high because of the distance, gently letting the drawn string pull the arrow from my fingers, I willed my arrow into his body as it made its swift flight.

As the arrow was reaching across the clearing, I knew I needed more practice. The light was such that I could see the flight of the shaft perfectly. I hadn't held high enough. I could see the arrow start to drop and go a little to the side. Instead of hitting him in the back like it was supposed to, he turned and it hit him squarely in the side of the butt, the left cheek to be exact.

While I was still watching the flight, I picked up and knocked another arrow. I took a quick aim and let it fly at Scar. The brave I'd shot squarely in the seat, jumped in the air, started to yell and dance about. It wasn't a fatal shot, but his days of chasing me were over. His days of sitting for a while were over, too. His main worry was keeping the wound plugged up so he wouldn't bleed to death. My second arrow missed Scar and I didn't wait to see what was going to happen. I knew he dove out of the way when the arrow lodged in the tree above his head. I turned around and vanished, running in giant strides over the gentle hills, avoiding groups of aspen and clumps of buck brush.

It would be a while before Scar was on my trail. Maybe he'd get slowed down by giving a fellow brave some help—and maybe not. I chuckled as I ran.

It's bad enough to be shot, but to be shot in the butt was the worst thing that could happen. At rendezvous, a bragging Frenchman and a trapper from Maine got in a scuffle. The American killed the Frenchie, but not before he let the Frenchie jam his Green River knife half way into his butt. No one remembered that the man from Maine fought well or that he killed the other man. All anyone could remember was his taking a knife stab in the rear end.

The brave who took my arrow had a painful wound and I felt kind of sorry for him, especially if the arrow got near the bone. Bone wounds are extra hurtful. But he was after me and I had to protect myself.

Now there was only one brave on my trail—Scar. But he'd be more careful and he knew that I was armed and wasn't shy about using force. I would get some distance between us to get him careless. Then it would be time I threw a little surprise party for Mr. Scar.

He'd been asking for an invitation and it was time he got it. I was going to even up the odds and I would do it the Rockwell way. I had a bag full of food, a good shirt on my back, moccasins on my feet—and something to fight with. When I found the right place, I'd know. Then I would even up the score.

CHAPTER 11

The odds were one-on-one, my kind of fighting numbers. I'll fight if I have to, but I don't like a community effort. I didn't think Scar could catch me unless I did something stupid and got myself boxed in a draw or twisted an ankle. But if I knew something of men, I knew he'd stay glued on my trail until I knocked on Brigham Young's front door. There would never be a moment's peace until Scar was out of the picture. I couldn't turn my back to him, enjoy an evening camp, knock off early, nor take an afternoon by a stream bank. He'd be stalking me like a buffalo wolf and I'd not get any rest.

He was mean, you can be sure. But the problem was I'd made him look bad in front of his people. Mighty Bear Claw hadn't let him balance up the scale since I took him down a few pegs. He sure came at me with blood in his eyes. The only thing that would even up the score now would be my hair dangling from his war lance.

I'd been inconsiderate, going off and making the shame worse because I'd not been easy to run down. His only hope of dignity among his tribe was bringing in my pegged-out hide.

The Crows, being the fighting men they were, would have admired my ability to get away. At the same time, my escape would reflect badly upon my pursuers, especially Scar. A Crow with lost honor was a Crow trying to gain it back. He had a lot to win by catching up with me, especially since I'd read from the book to his fellow braves. If he could get me, especially after I'd taken out the other warriors, he'd again be big medicine.

The trail got rougher as I made my way into the southern part of the Wind Rivers Range. If I kept going straight, I'd be hitting a large lake Fremont had found. It was near the headwaters of the Green. I planned to cut south before I got to that point, slipping across the more open country until I got down near Bridger.

But what to do with Scar?

He was starting to give me a headache and I had to deal with him or I'd make one small slip and he'd have me. Scar wouldn't fall for just any trap. The brave was smart and had more than his share of luck. I'd have to be canny to lay a trap for him, being very careful he didn't suck me into a trap of his own. Crow warriors were mighty cagey, good at seeing a likely ambush and turning the netter into the netted. I'd heard a lot of stories about mountain men trying to get one up on an Indian over a long winter. It didn't always have a happy ending.

As I climbed higher it got chilly. I passed a lot of snow packs in the shade. On the lee side it was sometimes four or five feet deep. I stayed on the spines of the ridges where it was clear, knowing full well in this type of country it was too muddy to worry about hiding sign. My best defense was a swift pace and a careful eye—being wary about getting trapped. In the late morning, I crossed a high mountain pass filled with snow. In these spring conditions, the snow looked none too stable. In fact it scared me in a bad way. I was nervous as I worked my way down that back face, wanting to get out of there fast but knowing I had to take it slow. I'd seen avalanches and what they'd done. This patch of snow was just waiting for someone to put his weight in the wrong place and trigger a slide.

If I lost my footing while I crossed this steep slope, I'd never need to worry about Scar. I'd be sliding into rocks that looked like they'd been sharpened on an Arkansas whetstone.

Once my lance saved me from a long slide. When my moccasins hit a bit of ice under the soft melt, my legs slid out from under me. At first I thought the whole mountainside was moving, but it was just me. I was about to be a human sled on a one-way ride. I slammed the shaft down, point first. It bit into the snow and ice and held me. I'd been lucky and checked myself before I'd gone a few feet. It took about forty-five minutes to get across onto solid rock. Even though it was mighty cool, I was covered with sweat. I was never so glad to get to solid mother earth.

Going down the west side of the slope was easy since there was little snow. I made good time, dropping what must have been more than three thousand feet. I reached a small mountain valley clogged with diamond willows and choke cherry. I crossed it and started up a steep canyon that rimmed a river.

After an hour, I'd found the right place to lay my trap for the man who wanted to see me scalped. By the end of this day, one of us might be dead. I'd been following a game trail up the steep canyon, startling a bunch of big horn on one turn. The river below me was swift, a dirty chocolate brown, swollen with run off. I didn't stop to look the place over since I wanted my sign to look like I was still moving. I could see up ahead where the trail curved—a good place to double back to lay and wait. I'd passed a lot of places a man could ambush his tracker; places that would make Scar wary. After a while, since nothing had happened, my hope was that he'd get a little complacent.

The afternoon breeze was stiff and cool, keeping me from sweating. The sun was warm in the sky and at the pace I was moving, it was easy to get overheated otherwise. I stopped and drank often and put dried meat in my mouth every hour or so. On one sunny slope, a few wildflowers were starting to bloom. When I reached a sharp turn in the trail about a quarter mile away, I cut back across the slope and waited in a small depression near the steepest part. Scar would be winded after climbing up the incline and I'd take aim as he stopped to catch his breath where it flattened out.

Being masked on the downhill side by a large clump of buck brush, I was pretty well hidden and could see anyone coming long before they got there. I took out two arrows and laid them on the ground in front of me. I loosened my knife in its sheath a few times so she would come out fast and smooth. Not knowing how long I'd have to wait, I took a drink in some run off and ate the last of Dull Horn's dried meat. I was glad I still had plenty of my own.

A man doesn't want to get full—he only wants to take the edge off his thirst and hunger. I'd like to have taken a nap. White fluffy clouds drifted by, driven by some fierce wind high above me. I kept a close eye on the trail, but I enjoyed a pair of whistling rock chucks on the talus where the slope got steep. Several thick pines seemed to grow out of mid air, gripping the edge of the canyon. At times when the wind died, I could almost hear the sound of the running water below me. Up the trail where I'd circled back, a cow elk and her calf were grazing, seeming not to have a care in the world.

It's amazing what you see when you sit down and look for a long time. I glimpsed a moving black spot on the slope across the canyon that must have been a black bear filling up on the spring grass. Not all the black bears you see in this part of the Rockies are black. Many of them have blond or sandy-red fur. I could have sat there all day and looked at the slope coming alive in the warm spring. I didn't let it carry me away, though. When the shape of a man rounded a turn a good half-mile off and start trotting up the slope, I forgot about what I'd been enjoying. I was thinking of only one thing and that was getting Scar off my back trail.

This man had been my nightmare. I couldn't keep moving with him following me—at least I couldn't keep moving freely. We had to settle this thing now. I was going to let him get right on me and then let rip with an arrow. I had another one handy, just in case. A sharp point where he lived would solve all my problems. Still, when it came down to it, something inside me wouldn't let me ambush him with fatal force. I had to meet him face-to-face.

It wouldn't be too hard to lay and wait, putting an arrow through his chest as he came up the trail. But that would only solve half my problem. I needed to face him head on. I wanted Scar to see my face when I took him out. An ambush was too impersonal and this was a personal fight he'd called me to. I stepped out from behind a rock as he topped the hill. "Scar," I yelled at the top of my voice.

The sound echoed across the canyon and back in an unnatural way. He looked at me. He wasn't more than fifteen feet away and I had him dead to rights. My bow was drawn back, an arrow resting at full draw. He stood still. His grimace didn't change.

I relaxed the arrow part way.

In my best Crow I shouted a few things you couldn't say in any Mormon Sunday School. Then I said, "You and me enemies. You and me will fight man-to-man."

Keeping an eye on him, I relaxed my bow completely and laid it by the edge of the cliff. He took his bow off his back and laid it down, never taking his eyes off me. He smiled slightly. I actually saw his wicked eyes. The thing you noticed most about this man, other than his scar, was his squint. His eyes were a dull-gray in afternoon light. His lip curled, indicating he couldn't believe his luck, and if I wasn't mistaken, his scar turned a little whiter, accented by his bronze skin. Sweat was beading off his face and he was breathing deep to catch his wind.

He knew I could have had him cold when he topped the rise, running him through with an arrow in the brisket. But I'd set down my bow as a show of good faith. I didn't think there was much honor in him, unlike most Indians, who lived and died by a code that was more strict than most white folks live by. But I knew he appreciated the chance to fight me, honor aside. This was close. This was personal. There was no give or mercy in his face and I expected none. I knew he'd take me anyway he could. I had to be true to my own gifts and killing a man with his back turned, or taken unaware, wasn't my way. With Dull Horn I wasn't trying to kill him. I was just trying to get him out of the way.

This is what I wanted, to go for him toe-to-toe, the way it's done among men. Still, after I saw him so cock-sure, I wondered if I'd bitten off more than I could chew. He pulled his knife and I pulled mine. Then we started to circle and I wasn't paying much attention to the eagle that was flying about or to the bear across the canyon. I never noticed if the elk and her calf grazed across the way.

I was no longer fighting for honor; I was fighting for my life.

His first jab was quick, darting out like a fighter's jab. The edge of his blade barely missed my belly. He thought he had me and came in again with the same move. I had cleverly baited him with an opening, which almost cost me a knife wound and he fell for it. I danced to the side as his knife shot past me. About the time the stab had gone full course, I slipped my left about his wrist, crunching down like a vice under my arm while I pushed up on his extended elbow. The pain caused him to wince, so he dropped the blade. Still holding him I kneed him in the groin and rested the point of my knife on his cheek. His involuntary twist caused the edge of my blade to bite down, giving even more reason for his name.

I thrust him back and threw his knife out of the way. I sheathed my knife and let him have it under the chin as he was still staggering. Punching wasn't something most Indians were used to. I gave him a few more good blows, which he took well. He came back at me like a Texas thunderstorm. I gave him a what-for-all in the gut—a punch that should have floored him. Most braves aren't much for fist fighting, but Scar, he was different. He was experienced at white-man fighting. He must have spent some time with a trapper somewhere along the line. I'd heard some French trappers worked this area, living right along with the Crows. He didn't know any English, I was certain of that. I would have spoken French to him but I didn't know any, except the word rendezvous.

A beating would lower him a notch or two. I wanted to be the man to do it, but it wasn't going to be easy. Maybe I'd made a mistake not shooting him when I had the chance. I circled about him like a prairie wolf, feigned a right to his gut. He dropped his hand to shield my blow, so I caught him a hard left in the mouth. It was a punch guaranteed to shake loose a man's teeth. He took it, though. I'll give him that. He took it and kept coming. I let my guard down. He swung about with a sneaky kick that took me in the wind. After that kick, one of the best I'd ever seen, I was sure he'd spent some time with a Frenchman; they are good at fighting with their feet.

I saw his next kick coming and tried to back up, but didn't quite make it. I felt the knife-edge of his foot dig hard into my gut. It surely knocked every ounce of breath out of me. I was standing, but not by much. For an instant, Scar smiled, thinking he had me good. Faster than a preacher's hand, like the brisk leap of a mountain buck, he drove his body at me, letting me have what-for-all with two opened palms in the chest. I blocked his advance, but I fought to stay on my feet as I buckled backwards toward the edge of the canyon. I managed to stay up and, by a stroke of luck, ducked my head and dodged his next charge. He wanted me on the ground where the fighting was more in his favor.

He was a little too sure when he came at me this time. A few hits always sobered me up in a fight. He'd nearly knocked me down, but I'd gotten my second wind. I'd be aching tomorrow, but now I felt no pain. I'd seen him in action and withstood his blows. I knew I needed to be careful of his feet. Indians weren't supposed to fight this way, but someone had forgotten to tell Scar. He'd learned some nasty tricks . . . but he wasn't the only one. I knew what to expect from him now.

Scar signaled his punch and I saw it coming in, round-housed hard and slow. I blocked it with my left arm and smashed him a good one under his chin with a sweeping right. He backed up before

I could take him with my left, rolling out of the way like he knew what he was doing. He came in again low and sure, but I caught him with my leg and threw him to the ground with a slick move a French fellow had taught me. Two could play this kicking game.

He came at me with hatred in his eyes. For five minutes we fought bitterly, my breath coming in ragged bursts. Scar was tough and he knew some Mississippi fighting moves, but he wasn't as used to taking the physical abuse in a white man's fisticuffs. In his world, a five-minute fight was a long battle. In my world, it took five minutes to get warmed up.

I hate to say this, but I think he would have nailed me if he'd gotten me on the ground. He tried, how he tried, to tangle me in those leathery legs. But I had the edge in this stand-up fight as long as I could keep him away from the clinch. Indian boys wrestle from the day they crawl and they're hard to take in a hard-ground tumble. On the ground was one place I didn't want to be with this buck.

I feigned a right and he opened up. I smacked him a few solid punches in the breadbasket to get where he lived. He tried a forward kick, but I expected it, so I twisted to the side and clubbed him across the face with the back of my fist. It sounded loud, even on the cliff top with a spring breeze. He tumbled to the ground, almost inviting me to dive on him.

He got up, grunting something in Crow and came at me. I saw it too late. I took a pounding on my ear and cheek from a rock he had in his clenched fist. It sent me back, reeling. If I hadn't blocked part of that blow, I'd be tumbling down the canyon to the river with a caved-in face. I'd be buzzard bait. He swung both fists, rocks in both, and came again, trying to get in close so he could thump me or twist me in a greasy bear hug. I backed up to where I'd called him out to catch my breath. I collected myself for a moment, panting hard, trying to ignore the ache in the side of my head.

He stood there staring at me and I was gazing back. I'd made pulp out of his bottom lip. He was bleeding freely from a dozen cuts on his face. We seemed to come to what they call a Mexican standoff... at least for a moment. He loathed me. His eyes, usually dull, now blazed with hate and revenge. We just stood there peering at each other, never looking away for fear of giving the other an advantage. Then I saw it in his eyes. He moved his left hand down, snatching up his war lance. Without thinking, I dove for mine, struggling to my feet.

He wanted to change the rules.

I braced my feet, standing down his charge. I checked his first blow and managed to give him a solid hit in the chest about heart level with the backside of my lance. It threw him off a little. His thrust wasn't timed as well as mine since his grip was off. I was using my lance as a staff, the way they did in old England in the days of that fellow called Robin Hood.

He went for broke and tried a daring forward stab, coming in low and upward, intending to enlarge my belly button enough for a jack rabbit to walk through. It nearly worked. Turning to the side, I thrust out, pushing his lance back, letting his momentum carry him away. Scar stumbled and caught his balance on the edge of the lip. He turned, starting to lift his war lance up when I caught him across the face with a savage swipe. I swung again, hitting him above the ankle. Something gave in.

He toppled like a sack of flour, going over backwards off the rim of the canyon. He may have broken his leg. In fact, I think he did.

About ten feet down, he turned to face me, hunched down, pain written across his face. There was no sign of fear. He knew I had him again and he wanted me to make quick ends of it. He hated me more for it. He shouted something to me in Crow, but I couldn't tell what it was. My guess was the shock from that broken leg was still masking a good bit of the pain.

Scar held his chest out for me to run him through with my lance. I did think about it, but only for a second. I thought I'd take pleasure in killing this man, but when it came right down to it, I'd beaten him and that was enough. Killing him wouldn't prove anything I hadn't already proved.

When it looked like I wasn't going to kill him right off, he started to move down hill just slightly. My guess is he thought I was going to toy with him. So I just stood there and watched him squirm. He found a stick to use as a crutch and he was keeping a wary eye on me.

He tried to stand, but he just tumbled and started falling. It wasn't straight down like a cliff, but it was pretty steep. A man could go down it or climb up it if he was careful. There was some loose gravel, but it was mostly mountain grass. He fell back and slid on his back, which was a good thing since it was better than going down leg-first with a broken limb.

I stood there dumbly and watched him slide toward the river, holding a hand full of snow on the side of my sore face.

At the bottom, I saw him moving around. The fall hadn't killed him, but it hadn't done him any good either.

I sat by a rock for nearly and hour, sucking on some jerky, trying to get my energy and wind back. I needed to be moving on, but I still didn't have it in me. I must've dozed off. When I woke up the sun was in the western sky. I had about four hours of daylight and needed to be traveling.

I picked up Scar's knife and possible bag. I helped myself to his arrows, which weren't as well made as Dull Horn's, but they would certainly do. I broke his bow on a rock and carried his lance as I walked up the trail. In a mile or so, I'd break it and drop it over the canyon. I didn't want to leave it where one of my enemies could use it against me.

I'd fought the biggest battle of my life. I was happy to be alive but I felt a little let down too . . . and very tired. The breeze had stopped and the warm rays felt good as I walked. I could feel life coming back into me. There was one more chore I had to do.

I was going back to the Crows to get my furs back!

CHAPTER 12

I felt some relief, but I kept moving anyway. It wouldn't take long for mounted braves on sure-footed ponies to catch up. I didn't know how long the tribe would wait before setting off to see what had happened. I'd be caught in the open like the proverbial wolf on a frozen lake.

When I got to the top of the steep canyon, I started hopping across rocks, making my trail hard to spot. I went a ways, jumping around, veering off the path, climbing up the rocky face. No way they could climb this hill with ponies. A man needed to be half mountain goat to get over it.

I used to think Mrs. Rockwell didn't raise fools, but here I was making my way back to that Crow camp. I dared not go back the way I'd come, since I'd play into enemy hands. Being in the mountains a long time, I had a good idea about where I was and where their camp was. My plan was to cut across a stretch of hills to the north and make my way east to the foothills. I didn't think it would take that long.

Now that I had weapons and footwear, I'd be traveling in comfort. I kept climbing, trying not to think about what might happen if I misjudged a handhold, triggered a slide, or twisted an ankle. By the time I got to the summit, my breathing was coming hard and the air was thin and chilly. I took in deep lungfuls but it didn't seem to satisfy much. These mountains were steep and cold.

I was climbing up a southern exposure, so at least it was clear of snow, except on the top. Every few steps I looked back to see if I could spot anyone on my trail or down in the valley. I had a good view for miles and felt like a hawk looking down. As far as I could tell, I was the only one about. I worked my way across the peak and down to avoid a snowfield. I'd had my share of them. Dropping lower, I came to a valley that I think ran parallel to the one I'd crossed earlier, and I found a place to camp. It was getting dark and I was cold. I must have been camping quite a bit higher up than I was the night before. It was downright chilly.

Light was fading fast, so I quickly laid up a good supply of dried wood from deadfalls. My toes, when I curled them down, crunched on frozen blades of grass. I was feeling pretty safe, so I built a good-sized fire. Most of the blaze was hidden by the pine and rocks. With my knife, working within the light of the fire ring, I started laying in a supply of pine boughs. I made a bough bed about six inches deep. Then I wove a simple backstop for a lean-to fire reflector.

With my fire blazing, I crawled into my lean-to. My muscles started aching at the joints and seemed to throb. Gratefully, I could feed my fire without getting up. Eating some of my bear jerky, I drifted off. When I got cold, I woke up and fed the fire more, then drifted back to sleep.

I'd intended to get an early start the next day, but when the sun warmed everything up, I turned my shoulder skyward, catching the rays, and glided back to sleep. When I awoke next, the sun was straight up. I polished off more dried bear meat and wandered off to a stream and had a long drink. I soaked my feet in the icy water and dabbed some sap on the biggest cuts. Then I took another nap like a lazy house cat.

It was all catching up to me. Sleep was the medicine I needed.

I was worn down in the body and I was worn down in the mind. After the fight with Scar, it was like a dam had burst and all that I was holding in had leaked out. Any fool knows you can only run a bloodhound so long before you must rest him, and this old dog needed a rest. Without a blanket, sleep at night was a fitful thing since a man had to get up and tend to his fire every little while. In the afternoon sun, I slept as warm as a baby on a thick feather mattress.

The shadows were getting long on the trees when I woke again. I was refreshed, but a little sluggish. I pulled in a new batch of wood against the night and took a look at the coming evening.

Had a Crow come by he'd have had me cold. I'd have had my throat cut and my hair scalped off and never known it. Of course, if a man is going to get scalped, not knowing it would be a good thing. I was about through my dried meat and would have to hunt tomorrow. Maybe I could walk upon a bighorn or a deer. Otherwise, I'd have to take time to follow a game trail or wait at a crossing.

Sitting there, all comfortable and dumb-like, I watched the night drain all the color out of the evening. When the last bits of orange and yellow cloud fire had gone from the sky, the high wispy clouds took turns blocking the stars. I built up my warming fire again.

The air iced your lungs and almost hurt if you took it too deep. The stars littered the heavens like frog eggs on a dark velvet surface. I thought of those Sunday school lectures I'd heard about God and the making of man and earth. It was a sorry shame the Sunday school folks didn't take youngsters out to look at the nighttime sky in all its glory, which is a better sermon on God than all the dry lessons and scripture spouting ever thought of being.

God was out there. All you had to do was look up and find Him. He was smiling down at the Wind River Mountains—his finest creation, except maybe the Yellowstone country. Looking at His handy work was enough for me to be a believer, even if a lot of dust hadn't settled on me in church. God loved the mountains foremost and a lonely wanderer could see why. You never heard of those old prophets going off to a city. When God wanted to talk to a man, He invited him into His living room, the mountains. Moses, if I remember right, went high to get his ten rules.

I felt sleep call me strongly away from all this thinking. I heard the snap of the wood in the fire as the flames consumed it. The warm glow of the heat felt inviting while the hint of the wood smoke and pine acted on me like a good tonic. I fell into a deep sleep. I woke a time or two and put fuel on the fire, falling back to a dreamless slumber. When I awoke the sun was fully in my face. I was hungry and refreshed. I lay there in my pine bed and looked up.

It dawned on me that this was the first time in a long while I'd just let the day wash over me.

I finished off the last of my grizzly jerky, which I'd been

nursing to make it last. After a drink, I checked the fire to make sure it was out. Picking up my weapons, I moved off down the trail. I knew I should turn around and work my way down to Bridger, leaving well enough alone. But I was determined to get my truck back. It was the last thing they'd expect.

A sensible man wouldn't go and put his fool head back in the bear's mouth after he'd been lucky to get out alive the first time. But I'm a fool, so I made my way down to the valley floor. Compared to what I'd been through, this seemed like a May-day stroll since there was no one immediately on my back trail. I alternated between a fast walk and a slow run, covering a fair amount of ground by mid-afternoon. My belly was going to get hungry soon, so I directed my attention to hunting something down for dinner.

There were a lot of red willows about, thick clumps by the streamside. Looked like a likely place to stumble onto a moose or a deer. This was also a good place to walk into a bear and I'd had my share of bears for a while. I climbed a hill overlooking the willows in the stream bottom and sat there, watching all about carefully.

After a half hour, I saw a black patch that seemed to be moving in a small circle. It was a moose, unless I missed my bet. Now, a moose was a lot of meat and I couldn't use it all, but a hungry man can't be too choosy. I climbed down and started a stalk.

I circled around so I could move into the south breeze. Moose don't have that big ugly nose for nothing. They also have big old ears that can hear a blade of grass bend at a hundred yards. Walking on tiptoes, half expecting to stir out an angry silvertip, I parted the tender spring foliage with the tip of my bow, quiet as a stalking cat. There was an arrow in my left hand and a second in my teeth.

Peering about, the thick marshy grass softening my steps, I came upon the moose about twenty yards away. It hadn't seen nor smelled me. Hidden among the leaves, I anchored my arrow and let her fly. It struck home right in the lungs. In a heartbeat, I aimed a second arrow for the same spot. It struck a few inches from the first. I was doing some good shooting.

As often happens when you shoot big game with an arrow and they don't know you're about, the animal sort of looks up, wondering. It's like they were stung by a bee or bitten by a mosquito—they feel the arrow but don't know what to think. This moose, a yearling bull, looked up from his grazing, then went back to eating again. In less than a minute, he'd dropped dead.

I skinned him quick and pulled off those tasty back straps and moved into the woods to find a camp. I settled on a nice place with some water three hundred yards away. There was fuel for a cozy fire and a ledge that would reflect my blaze and keep off any rain in the night.

Getting a fire going, I made my sleeping pallet from evergreen boughs. Picking up my lance, I headed back to my kill where I got his hide and more of the best cuts. After I got my furs and such from the Crows, I'd be making a run for it. I wouldn't have time to stop and hunt, so I'd lay in a healthy supply of jerky now.

I figured I could be at the Crow's camp in two days. It would take me all of five minutes to get my truck, if things went well. Then I'd disappear. With a stroke of luck, I'd be ten miles gone before they discovered I'd taken anything!

There was still some light left, so I took a walk into the black-diamond willow stands and gathered an arm-load of finger-size saplings. I built together a first-rate meat drying rack about four feet high. From the larger pieces, I built the outside frame to attach the smaller sticks to. In the last light, I cut a few arm loads of spruce bows. Then I staked out my moose hide.

I started a bed of hot coals going in a shallow pit. Placing the willow drying rack over the pit, I started slicing up long thin strips of moose meat, placing them on the structure so close together they touched. As they dried, they'd shrink. After I got the meat in place, I built the coals up more so they gave off more heat.

I put the frame over my rack and wove the bows into the sides to help hold in the smoke and heat so the meat would cure faster. I labored over the coals a little more. Then I put on some wet wood to raise up a head of smoke. My make-shift smoke house would do just fine, and I'd have plenty of jerky by morning.

After that, I scraped a piece of moose hide I'd laid over a log. I used my knife and a flat rock. It was hard going, but it felt satisfying to work with my hands. I also started my dinner, slicing up thick sections of moose back strap, spearing them on some shafts of green willow and letting them sizzle above the coals.

Nothing tastes better than moose, unless maybe you've got some fresh mountain lion handy.

After a fine supper, I started to work on that hide. I boiled some of the moose brains and water in a dish-like rock. I rubbed the white paste onto the hide I'd scraped. Next, I rolled the hide to cure it. It was still mighty green. You need more time to do a proper job of brain tanning, but this would have to do. I would be needing some footwear and moose made a fine moccasin, probably the best. I'd scraped more than enough to make two pairs. I did some extra for good measure. You need to smoke your hide for a long while if you really want to do it right and get it waterproof, but I didn't have that luxury. If you were tepee living, you could leave the hide up near the top of the poles and get it cured just right. Under these traveling circumstances, I was glad to do what I was doing.

About every hour or so, I adjusted the meat on the racks so it would dry evenly. At the same time, I re-rolled the hide, making sure that the boiled brain got spread about evenly. All the while I kept eating fresh moose meat until I was stuffed as a Christmas goose.

I wasn't tired, so I worked on my bear claws. Up until now, I hadn't had a chance to do much with them. I fashioned them into a bear necklace.

A man couldn't help admiring such claws. They were three inches of furious death, enough to rip open a good size tree or tear out the throat of a cow elk. At the same time, I'd seen grizzly working some roots on the hillside. His claws were used almost like fingers on a human being. A grizzly necklace, especially if you killed it with your own hand, was a proud thing to have and wear. Hugh Glass, a famous mountain man from the early days, had himself such a necklace. They say he killed his bear with a butcher knife. Some questioned it, but none would doubt it to his face. It was said he'd eat a man alive if he had a mind to. For a while, he was set on finding Kit Carson, himself, to do him some personal harm. Rumor had it Glass was going after Kit for leaving him with a broken leg.

I never knew how much to believe when I listened to a mountain man yarn. Those old boys loved to tell stories. Anyway, it was before my time during the peak of the fur trade, days that are gone forever. I only wish I would have been in the Rockies when the beaver was king. Those must have been glorious times. And unlike now, when rendezvous is only a flash in the pan, back then it was a thing to see.

The West was changing and so were my mountains. Maybe

Canada would stay pure for a while—not so many people running about. They say a man can paddle a canoe for a few months at a time and not meet up with anyone if he'd a mind to.

Not far off I heard a wolf, then another answer. They'd likely come upon that moose, unless some bear was sitting on it. I enjoyed wolf talk. It was like symphony music to my ears. I built up the coals on my smoke hut. Then I added more dry wood. My moose jerky was curing up nicely.

I banked up my warming fire a little more, watching the moon wander across the night-time sky. I started to give some thought to how I was going to get my truck back. A man just doesn't waltz right into a Crow camp and walk away with his furs. Still, by the ghost of Hugh Glass, who they called Lord Grizzly, I was going to make those Crows pay for my inconvenience.

What I'd give to see the look on their faces when they found out they'd been had. It made me chuckle to think on it. I'd given my word I'd bring back furs and I'd do it. Folks were counting on me.

About midnight with my necklace nearly done, I stoked my fire. Putting some elbow grease into it, I stretched my scraped moose hide on a thick tree branch. Once it was good and stretched, I worked it back and forth to soften it. After that, I squeezed all the moisture out. Then I hung the moose hide in my makeshift smoke hut to cure it some. I crawled into my evergreen bed and watched the stars, smelling dried meat mingled with drying moose skin. I looked at the dipper and that was all I remember until the cold night woke me. I built up my fire again, enjoying the warmth of the yellow-orange blaze. I should have rotated my drying meat, but I was too tired. After throwing on wood, I slept until dawn, waking to build the fire again—almost an eternal task in the mountains, it seemed.

I was going back, but I wasn't that anxious to leave my snug little camp. I'd built my traveling moccasins. They're called that because you make them while you travel and they're not as good, nor do they last as long, as the kind you'd make otherwise. I finished drying my meat. I finished my necklace. I put it on and wore it proudly.

It must have been near mid-morning before I got on the trail. My claws rode handsomely on my neck—although they bit into my skin when I moved the wrong way. My possibles bag was stuffed with dried meat, as was part of a legging. I had what was left of the back strap wrapped in leaves in the other legging. Both were flung over my shoulders like leather tubes.

I'd recovered both arrows from the moose, so I was stocked. With two knives, a bow and a lance, I was ready to face what needed to be faced. I was entering Crow hunting grounds and could, at any time, stumble upon unfriendly faces. They ate more than buffalo, enjoying elk and moose. These valleys were first-rate hunting grounds.

I'd mask my trail, you can be sure. And I'd go softly keeping an eye out for trouble.

I was walking into a hornet's nest.

Chapter 13

I felt rested.

Feeling like a good run, I settled into a brisk pace and started to burn up some miles, drifting gradually downhill, working the laziness out of me. When I felt myself start to get winded, or I was beginning to go up a grade, I'd slow down until my breathing got regular again. Doing this, I could keep moving for a long time without resting.

I wasn't sure how to make my approach, but working my legs helped keep my mind active. Seemed reasonable that no matter how you stacked it, they wouldn't plan on my returning. Still, I had some choices. I could push farther north and sneak up the trail they'd brought me in on as a captive. I could drift south and hit the trail I'd run the arrow on. Or, I could push east, bushwhacking my way in across country.

Giving it considerable thought, the sweat glistening on my

brow as I trotted, I decided not to drop south on account of my likely meeting up with a scouting or a hunting party. If I went north I might overshoot the trail all together. Being pretty sure of my direction, I'd keep pushing east, but I'd be moving wary, you can bet on that.

It was a little past noon when I saw him off in the distance, sort of stumbling across the meadow.

I'd hardly noticed him. I'd gotten so complacent. Like my old preacher used to say, I hardly noticed there was a snake in the grass . . . or the devil around every bend waiting to take me unawares and lead me down to fiery blazes. At first I thought it might be a trap, a lone man like that, but then I came to realize no man can act that good. He just staggered, fell down and got up. Then he fell, face-first. He got up again. He had pluck, I can tell you that.

Moving careful-like, using the brush to shield me, an arrow knocked, I circled to where I was fifty yards in front of him. He was flat on the ground again, so I didn't recognize him—other than he was an Indian. But as he lifted himself by his elbows and struggled to his knees before dropping again, I knew who he was.

It was Dull Horn.

He had a fair share of courage, I'll give him that. How he got this far—busted head and an arrowed leg wound—was a mystery to me. I went over to see what I could do. He was out of his head with fever, I could see that plainly. His forehead was hot as a June bride. He was a mess and I knew I had to help him best I could.

Dull Horn was all dirty. Dried vomit covered the front of him. He smelled fierce, having thrown up. That often happens with head wounds. Before I did anything, I led him to a beaver dam about forty yards off the trail and pulled off his clothes. Then I led him to the edge and he stumbled in. The water was about knee high, so stripping off my footwear and rolling up my pants, I gave him a washing. I rinsed out his clothes, then bathed his head, which was burning up. I also washed out his hair with sand and water to get out the sour-vomit smell which is something I can't abide. I'd rather smell rotting bear grease.

I threw his clothes on a few willows to dry in the breeze. After he was cleaned up and cooled down, I led him to some tall grass, keeping a wet compress on his forehead. Sitting in the cool water and the compress had done him some good. Seemed his fever was lowered a little.

He wasn't the best fighter, but he was a man. It took some kind of courage to stay alive this long, being out of his head like he was. But it also got me worrying.

I thought one of the braves would have helped him back. Maybe he was never found. Had they split up and not rendezvoused looking for me? Had they passed Dull Horn, not seeing him since he was wandering about fever drunk? The real question I had was whether someone was on my trail even though it was a few days old?

Was someone closing in on me now?

Maybe I was lucky someone hadn't lifted my hair when I slept. Stroking my bear claw necklace, I wondered. Dull Horn was a tough man and I thought he'd live, but not without my help. He must have wandered off in a haze, drifting north. That also meant he'd come through a valley since he was in no shape to climb over the high stuff.

While he was lying naked on the buffalo grass, I checked his leg. He was mumbling something that sounded like Raven Woman, if my Crow was right. She must have been his wife. I think he thought I was her. The wound on the back of his leg had festered bad. The entry at the front was looking okay. I cleaned them both with warm water—burns are nasty-looking but the fear of infection was troubling my mind more. I chewed up a wad of aspen bark for a packing and covered it with leaves, binding it in with some moose hide. Aspen helps things heal.

Then I cleaned his feet. They were gashed and cut up since I was wearing his footwear. I was getting pretty good at foot care these days. I washed and cleaned the cuts and made a poultice of aspen leaves and bark for them.

In the meantime, from my moose jerky, I was making broth. From a two-foot square piece of moose hide, I made a cooking pouch. It's called paunch cooking by the mountain men, who, I think, learned it from the Sioux. You take about four sticks and lash the top. Then you pull the legs out so it looks like you have a three or four-foot tepee frame. Following that. you lash a corner of the hide to each stake.

When that was done, I shaved off jerky and added water. With some willow tongs, I took hot rocks out of my fire and dropped them into the water. After the rocks heated the water, I pulled them out and dropped in a few more until I had a boil going and a fine moose broth stewing in my hide cooking pan.

It's a long process, but it works. I use a paunch because I never could figure out how the old timers made a cup from bark. I guess you could do it from quaking aspen, but I believe birch bark would be best since it's thinner. There was no birch around here that I knew of.

By afternoon, Dull Horn's clothes were dry and I dressed him against the night. Evenings get cool, and how he managed to survive this long without freezing to death will always be a mystery to me. He must not have been out of his head the whole time since

I noticed he'd polished off that pemmican I left him.

Propping him up, I bound his head and made him drink some broth. For the first time, he looked at me, but there didn't seem to be fear. I wondered if he was awake enough to know I'd helped myself to his bow?

Where we were was too marshy for an overnight camp. The coolest temperatures always seem to settle in the valley bottoms anyway. It's not a problem if a man's got blankets and truck, but it is when you don't even have a coat. Up a draw and by the side of a fallen tree, I set up camp. I got a fire started and wood in about the time the sun was starting to set. I went back and got Dull Horn and, with his arm over my shoulder, I carried him back to our camp.

Fashioning a tight lean-to of spruce with a thick mat of boughs and pine needles, I laid him down. The sky looked threatening, so I added more layers to the lean-to making it water tight. There wasn't much else to do, so I drug in wood until the first clap of thunder rolled across the evening sky.

We were in for a Wind River thunderstorm. It might last for twenty minutes or for three days. Well, we were settled and snug. I propped up Dull Horn again and gave him some broth. Then I had some myself. I took the last of my fresh moose and laid it on a flat rock to broil.

The thunder was so loud it seemed to make the boulders rumble. At times the earth shook mightily and I wished I had a door between me and the night. The rain was coming down like it was being poured from a hog's head. The fire was spitting and snarling, but was burning. I took another drink of broth and went to give Dull Horn another sip, but he was fast asleep. Sleep and a little food would do him good. He hadn't had much of either in the last few days.

One thing for sure, in this rain, any trail we'd made would be washed out. This was the kind of rain that made Noah glad he had him an ark. For a moment I wondered about Scar and hoped he was as miserable as I was dry and comfortable.

Dull Horn turned and I saw that he was awake.

I gave him another drink of the jerky soup which was cool by now. He took it eagerly and finished it, then drifted back to sleep. I lay down, knife in hand, shutting my eyes.

By morning the rain hadn't let up.

For the rest of the day, I fed Dull Horn broth and bits of boiled meat. He mostly rested. I stayed pretty snug since I wasn't a duck or a beaver. I was pretty bored just sitting there. But at least I was dry. A few times the rain let up and I scooted off to the thickets for wood.

I reflected it was an interesting twist of fate. Here I was saving the life of the man I'd fought in combat. What was more, it was my sworn Christian duty and I could do no less. I was pleased to help.

Rest and food did Dull Horn a wagon load of good. These Indians heal fast from wounds that might kill or lay up white folks for a fortnight. The next day I helped him along over the steep stuff, but he hobbled about as sure as a day-old colt. We didn't talk too much at first, not that I could have carried on a long discussion anyway. What was there to say?

At first I was afraid to turn my back.

I didn't know if he'd come down on my head with a club. He already knew what a rock would do. I found he bore me no ill will that I could tell, even if I was the one who bumped him and arrowed his leg. He seemed to accept it as if it was decreed by that

Great Spirit of his. I'd won fair and square. And sure as shooting, I'd saved him, and he knew it.

That was all he needed.

I told him as best I could that I'd take him back to his camp and his people. It seemed to please him and he smiled at me as if we were life-long blood brothers.

You couldn't help liking him.

He was one of those sorts that, no matter what the color of his skin, he was likeable. Now, I'll admit until now I never much thought of a Crow as likeable. I respected them, yes. But *like* wasn't a word a man in this country usually used to describe a tribe of folks who seemed hellbent fierce.

I was up front, telling him I was going back to his camp to get my truck. "A man shouldn't be left without his horse and guns in this country," I told him squarely. "I mean to have my furs and, like as not, a few extra horses for my trouble."

He gave me a toothy grin and said a few things I couldn't quite make out. I didn't ask for clarification. He told me something else I did catch.

"You're a great runner," he said in earnest. "You're good on the trail, good as the best man from my clan. It would have been a great honor to take you. It's been many winters since a white man ran the arrow without being caught. There's never been a white eyes in my time who escaped running."

Looks like you caught me, I was thinking. There was more than one way to be caught.

He said something like Fast Deer Feet and tried to dance a lick, but his hurt leg wouldn't allow him. He whooped a mighty chant and sang something. I didn't know it, but from that time on, my name would be Fast Deer Feet. Sometimes you're better off not fighting a name. I accepted my new handle with honor and that was that. I supposed I'd get a good chuckle over it later.

I wondered why my going back to get my truck never bothered Dull Horn. He took it as natural as could be. It was as if every day you took a man's gear, tried to run him down and kill him. Then when he outwitted you, you let him take back the things you took in the first place. You can never figure out an Indian, if you're brought up white, no matter how hard you try.

He noticed I had weapons, his lance, bow, and knife. But he hadn't said anything until afternoon. He pointed to the bow, which was relaxed and on my back. He pointed at it again, drawing my attention to it.

"Fine bow. Very fine bow!" he said proudly. "Best bow in clan. True bow."

I pointed to my bear claw necklace and said. "Yes, good bow. I kill big bear with bow and arrow." I cleverly omitted that I was chased up a tree first and the bear took a while to die. I could tell he was impressed.

"Bow in hands of Fast Deer Feet. Great warrior for great bow. Never let Scar have bow. He wanted bow."

I said a few things about Scar you'd dare not say in at a prayer meeting. Then Dull Horn looked keenly at me while I paused at a hilltop. "Fast Deer Feet has the knife of the man with a scar on his face. He not give you knife?"

In my best Crow, I tried to make him understand. I'm not sure he understood all the details, but he got the general idea about what happened. I pointed over the range I'd just crossed.

"He have black spirit," Dull Horn said. "Many in clan like him little. But he be brave warrior. He wants in his heart," he pointed to his heart, "to be large chief."

Dull Horn looked off toward the east as if he knew exactly where camp was. "His heart has shadows. Mighty Bear Claw knows it. It is good a great warrior fight him. You took his hair? Where is it."

"He's still alive," I said.

"That be not good," he exclaimed. "Fast Deer Feet should have sent his spirit."

"Maybe he's dead," I said. "He's as bad off as you were, or maybe he was worse. If he lives, he'll have to live with the fact I bested him two times. Everyone else will know it. Hope it shames him. I know I broke his leg."

We walked on in the soft breeze. In the afternoon we were crossing a long marsh. It was filled with waterfowl. At one point Dull Horn asked for my knife which was a loco thing to do, almost as loco as me handing it over. He got down on his knees and started digging some tubers in the soft earth. He washed them off and patted his stomach. There was some quacking through the bushes, so I knocked an arrow. He touched my shoulder and shook his head, Dull Horn picked up a number of fist-sized rocks and crept forward.

He let go and there was a bunch of flapping in the shallow water. Then he let go again. Jumping in that swamp, he had us two birds by the neck and was flipping them around his head wringing their necks.

Come evening we roasted those ducks that he'd chocked plumb full of tubers. It was all mighty tasty and a welcome change. I'm not sure what those tubers were, but they were as close to fresh vegetables as I'd had in a coon's age. The way I ate, you'd have thought I was polishing off a Sunday dinner.

He wasn't as used to eating as I, so I finished off what he didn't eat. And he was pleased to give it to me, too. I'd grown to like this man. He wasn't a slacker. When we made camp, he didn't wait to be told to collect wood or boughs for the nighttime beds. I wasn't worried about him running off. Not that I couldn't catch him with his bum leg.

I learned something about him as we travelled toward his village, piecing things together. I found he was noted for making bows, which I'd already guessed, but he was skilled as a hunter. When he was nine winters, he made his first bow and threw a stalk into a small herd of buffalo. Sneaking up within a few feet, he let his arrows fly. That day he killed three head, quite a few for a boy. The tribe was grateful. This was how he got named Dull Horn.

When he was a year older, he crept up on a wolf and shot it cold. Before he was twelve, he'd killed all the beasts of the forest and plains except for the great bear—which would come later. While he was a great hunter and a craftsman, he wasn't noted as a warrior. Dull Horn had little interest in fighting men. He'd rather hunt. While this could pose a problem for a young man, he was so skilled at hunting and at making bows it never seemed to matter to his clan. He was a valuable man to have around.

Now and then he was required to go on a war party, which he usually turned into a hunting trip. On many cold winter days, he'd bring in the food to feed the hungry.

He wasn't modest about his skills, but he wasn't bragging either. It was down-home, straight talk. He knew what he could do and he did it! He'd gone along on the run because the elders had asked him to. He was the best tracker of the bunch and he'd have the best chance of keeping me tracked down. He was the first one on my trail. The tribe was worried that Scar would be too eager and lose my sign.

He spit when he spoke of Scar. I spit just to be polite. Scar was old pond scum in my book. I was learning a lot about the mountains from Dull Horn. One thing I learned was a man could eat more than just red meat if he'd a mind to.

Dull Horn knew every trick. He showed me places to find duck eggs in the marsh. He pointed to plants a man could eat that weren't half bad. Those tubers he dug out of the marshes were good. They were a cross between potatoes and turnips. They weren't as good as your ma's mashed 'taters with cream and butter, but they weren't bad at all.

On the morning of the fourth day, Dull Horn put his hand on my shoulder and said, "Fast Deer Feet brother to Dull Horn."

He asked for my knife and I gave it to him, although I kept a careful eye. He took his right palm and pushed the end of the blade into the pad until a small streak of blood ran from the cut. He pointed to my right hand and handed me back my knife. I dug the dull blade into my palm until I had a stream of blood running down my wrist. My blood seemed to flow easier because my cut was bigger.

With his left hand, he brought my hand to his. We clasped hands in the breeze. I looked down into the mountain valley below and up at the mighty peaks to the east. A hawk screamed in the blue sky above my sight. He held my hand with his, high above our heads as if he were trying to have us reach one of the clouds drifting by in the lazy breeze. For the longest time we held our hands up. He chanted something in Crow, something about mingled blood between the Crow clan and the white man.

"We be brothers now!" He shouted to the sky. "Fast Deer Feet have the blood of a human being, the blood of a Crow."

Dull Horn took off his bone tube necklace, accented with red and blue trade beads, and sat down on the dry earth. He motioned for a knife and I gave him his and told him to keep it. I would use Scar's. He smiled at me and motioned for me to sit also. I did.

He quickly made two strands from the bone and beads, connected by sinew, making two identical necklaces—one for each blood brother. Before he was finished, I took my grizzly bear claws necklace, which I wasn't wearing at the time, and pulled off two claws, one for each strand. Dull Horn looked pleased. In a few moments, a bear claw was hanging from the center of each. I proudly tied mine on my neck while Dull Horn tied on his.

"Blood brothers," I said in a firm voice. "Blood brothers," I shouted at the blue sky in Crow.

I felt flattered—the way you feel when you shoot the head off a turkey at a shooting contest.

"We be in camp before the moon rises two times," he said.

Fine, I thought.

Chapter 14

With a wobbly hand, Dull Horn pointed northeast to a notch in the ridge. "Clan several hours' walk beyond," he said as his face tightened up.

The notch looked like a small valley between some rocky rises, and as best as I could figure, it might be about five or six miles away. It appeared to be pretty easy walking, too, since it didn't look like we'd have any big hills to go over. Dull Horn looked worn down since morning. I slowed my pace. He was shying away from me helping him. He had his pride. All along I'd been thinking about going back to that camp and how I'd do it. Was I going to leave Dull Horn a few miles away and sneak in? Or was I going to boldly walk into camp and take what was rightfully mine? Not only did my horses and truck represent all my worldly possessions, I needed the cash money from the sales of my furs. There were lots of folks counting on me so they'd be warm the following winter, especially if Brigham Young sent a group of his Mormon saints into the Cache Valley to set up another settlement. He had plans to spread out all over the Great Basin and no one could talk him out of it.

Talk was the Cache Valley might be cold for flatland farmers, but it was a pretty place. No matter how you looked at it, most any place in the Great Basin was cold come wintertime and what the folks needed was some of my furs. It was my guess Ol' Brigham wouldn't send his folks to the Cache just yet. There were too many other places down lower they could move into.

So what was I to do?

A sane man wouldn't be living in the Rockies by himself and loving it. Of course I prided myself on not being sane. I gave what I was going to do a powerful amount of thinking as I was walking. Crows, like all Indians, respected a brave more than anything else. Often a man who rode alone into a camp or toward a band of braves, even if they were on the prowl for scalps, would be allowed to come in . . . and ride out. They rewarded courage. Still, I'd been in the mountains enough to know that Indians were whimsical.

After walking a few miles on the trail, I felt something was wrong so I turned about. There he was, just lying in a heap a couple of hundred yards back. When I ran to him, I found his breath coming short. He could barely talk. I pulled him over against a rock and cupped some water from a nearby creek with my hands. He took a few sips. I wiped the rest on his brow, a fevered brow and that worried me. I pulled off his bandages since I wanted to take a look at what was underneath. As I suspected, he wasn't healing up.

I should have let him rest more. We'd moved too soon.

He looked up at the sky limply. Then he went flat on me.

We'd been talking as we walked. Then he went kind of silent.

I thought he ran out of words. That should have been a clue.

His head wound looked as good as you might expect, but the wound on the back of his leg looked plenty bad. It looked to me like the burn was festering. It was red and hot to the touch and was oozing all sorts of stuff that couldn't be good. Being weak like he was, his body could only do so much healing up. In the last day, most of his body energy went toward walking and not getting over his wounds. I cursed the fact we didn't have mounts. If we had horses, he'd probably be alright.

I was worried, but I didn't have time to fret since I had to move fast to save him. I started up two cook fires as quick as I could and got them burning mighty hot. I pushed a healthy amount of heating rocks in since I had to do some serious boiling.

Hanging a couple of hide pouches between some small tepee-framed sticks, I filled the moose skins with water—carrying water back and forth from the stream in my moccasins. I cleaned up his wounds the best I could with what we call Missouri gourd or soap plant. It's found in dry soil and it smells something like garlic. It's a coarse looking vine with yellow flowers, but when you crush it up in water it makes a soapy lather that cleans up skin as good as soap. I soaked Dull Horn's festering leg a little, then I cleaned it up some more with that Missouri gourd soap, getting it as clean as I could. With a patch of moose skin, I made warm compacts and let them sit on his wounds while I went looking for the plants and herbs I needed—medicines I need to turn the festering.

I was going to make a poultice. I could hear Dull Horn mumbling something while I worked. He was out of his head. He'd gotten that way in a hurry, which surprised and troubled me. I could have sworn he was on the mend. I collected root bark off a large cottonwood tree growing nearby. I boiled it for some time until it was all mushy. Then I took it out and smashed it on a flat rock and chucked it back into the boiling water. Cottonwood doesn't work as well as slippery elm, but it was the best I could do here. I bound up his other wounds with barky mush for good measure, but I put an especially big dose on the back of his festered leg. According to mountain folk, boiled cottonwood bark soothes the tissues, especially on a burn, helping to keep it from getting more infected. I hoped it worked.

While working on his wounds, I was brewing up a powerful batch of quinine tea. Quinine brush grows all over and I thanked the good Lord I was able to find some without much looking. In fact, I couldn't have picked a better place had I scouted out the whole valley. This tea is made from an evergreen shrub. It has tassel-like clusters hanging all about. She's a mighty bitter plant, but it's good for fevers. You can't brag on the taste. I've tried it a few times when I was sick, myself. After making the tea, there wasn't much else I could do.

He needed help but I'd done all I could.

The Indians weren't doctors, but they had better ways of fixing hurts than I had. I didn't have much choice now. I had to get Dull Horn into his camp where he could get fixed up by someone who knew more than me. As fast as this had come on him, I knew he might die. That would pain me. I liked him and wasn't ready to wish him off to his Happy Hunting Ground. Besides, we were blood brothers. He was just a regular man like me, once I got to know him. I felt a little bad that I'd been the cause of all this. However, under the circumstances, I'm not sure fate gave me much choice. It's kind of funny, in a sad way, that I would end up trying to dent the skull of a man I'd want to go hunting with if I had taken the time to get to know him.

Dull Horn needed help from his people or he was going to go under fast. I knew what I'd do. I was going to take him to his village. With strips of moose hide from the cooking paunch, I lashed together a travois with a make-shift seat and had Dull Horn lay back on it. With the poles under my arms, I started dragging him back toward his village. I tied my bow and lance to the travois so I wouldn't have to fight with them. Since he was going from hot fever to cold chills, I put the leather shirt back on him. It was going to be hot business for me with all that pulling, anyway.

I got a quick appreciation for folks using hand carts. Pulling was hard work and I'm not ashamed to say it. Of course they had wheels on their carts, but they were carrying heavier loads.

I was lucky the going across wasn't steep or it would have taken twice as long. Three or four times I had to stop and retie my lashings which had stretched out because the leather was green. Twice he came out of his fever enough to give me a few directions, so I wouldn't have to take one step more than necessary. Apparently, this was familiar ground.

Many thoughts were romping about my head. Mostly I was more worried about my friend than I was about walking into a tribe of Crows that last week had taken delight in running me down. I wanted to stop and brew him another cup of tea to try to take the edge off his pain, but I thought it best to keep moving.

What I wouldn't have given for a good horse right now. For that matter, I'd have been happy for any horse, even a worn out plow nag. My muscles ached.

A gust of wind blew a dust devil in front of me, which is rare for this time of the year. I watched it go about two feet without interest as it disappeared into a clump of spring-green buffalo grass. The tops of the lodge pole pines swayed back and forth like mad dancers in the stiff afternoon breeze. I left the trees and came across the plain. The sweat dried on my neck. At least the wind was at my back.

My shoulders and arms ached from the long poles. I'd paced myself, as any man would have to, but I hadn't stopped to rest since I'd begun. Dull Horn had passed out several times and was still fevered up. There was nothing more I could do for him, except get him to some help as fast as I could. I hoped his people would know what to do. He was too good a man to let fade into the other world and I was feeling bad that I'd run that arrow through his leg.

Dull Horn was the kind of man you'd like to ride the river with. He was solid and true. Other than Left Foot's woman, this was the first time I'd come face-to-face with Crows where I could get to know them, and in spite of what they'd put me through, I had to say I liked them. I felt a kinship with Mighty Bear Claw, but I was feeling a brotherly bond to Dull Horn—especially since all my family was gone. Sometimes you don't have to travel a road with a man very long to feel you've known him all your life. It surprised me that someone could feel like kin so fast to a man that wasn't the same race.

I was learning a few things and I'd discovered most of those social fences we set up were only in our head. There wasn't much real about them. When it got down to it, people were people. Some were good and some were bad. Some you liked and some you didn't. If I had to walk myself to exhaustion to save Dull Horn, I'd do it.

For the second time in less than a week, I was going to enter the Crow village. I could see the cone-shaped tepees in the distance and the smoke from the cook fires bending in the wind before I could smell them.

An Indian camp has a unique smell to it, one you never forget. It's not unpleasant, but it's different from the smell of a white man's town, which has an odor to it, too. An Indian town smells like half-burned buffalo chips, partly cured hides, rancid grease and drying meat all at once. It's a comforting smell, I'm told. I've heard a man with a good nose could smell a camp several miles away in a gentle breeze, but I'm not sure I believed it. But you could scent a camp if you were downwind some.

I took a deep breath of Indian camp and tightened up my hold on the two poles. I was coming in from the west. When I looked off to the north, I could see the long hill I'd ridden down as a captive. It seemed almost a lifetime ago. So much had happened in the last few days, a man felt as if he'd aged some. The lines on my face were now battle scars I'd carry proudly—my lips split from the dry wind, my face and neck burned red. The cuts on my feet were healing up since I had something to cover them, and the goose egg on my head was gone and you couldn't feel it.

I was tired but wasn't about to let the Crows see that. I was afraid, too, but I wasn't about to let them see it. Squaring my shoulders proudly, adding a little vigor to my step, I ignored the ache in my arms and chest. I walked proudly forward. I wanted these folks to see a man coming in, proud and brave as if it were the most natural thing you could think of. As Left Foot said, "You had to show no fear even if you were bobbing at the knees and ready to pee your buckskins."

Chapter 15

I didn't know the signal for entering the Indian camp, nor would I have used it if I had known. In just a minute they'd see me, if they hadn't already.

Three small, bare-footed boys were hunting down a jackrabbit in the tall grass with throwing sticks and blunt arrows. They were so intent upon their prey, they failed to see us until we were nearly upon them. After standing there watching for a long moment, not sure what to do, they forgot the bewildered rabbit and ran off toward the camp shouting something I didn't understand.

When I was several hundred yards from the ring of tepees, a few braves were pointing my way and calling. In no time, a half dozen well-armed braves were walking toward us holding war lances or clubs.

Any tribe on these plains was always ready for war and sudden attack. They didn't have to stop and debate an issue that might look threatening. They just reacted. A few braves walked toward me, but I knew a full complement of armed warriors was waiting around the tepees for a quick show if needed. It took just a few seconds for the tribe to get ready.

Careful eyes were peeled in all directions lest it be some sort of a trick to draw their attention away from a main attacking body. A clan with this many horses had to be on guard every moment since they were a ripe target for plunder. Letting down their guard for even a few minutes could mean death or capture, or at the least, the loss of their horse herd which was considerable. The life blood of buffalo hunting tribes was its horses and they are jealously guarded. Of course, the fact that the Crows stole most of their horses from raids on other tribes wasn't a consideration.

The warriors, none I recognized, stood in front of me. I didn't stop. They parted and I went among them and they walked beside me, weapons gripped, ready for action. It was obvious that I was bringing in one of their own.

One short, stocky brave with a red blanket wrapped about his shoulders, an eagle feather dangling from his hair, pointed to my necklace and the identical one on Dull Horn. "We are blood brothers," I said without thinking. "Get out of my way!"

He said something to the others, but I wasn't able to make it out with my fledgling Crow and the scraping drag of the poles on the ground.

Before we got to the first circle of tepees, more braves came forward. One of them was Mighty Bear Claw. He had a puzzled look on his face, but it seemed to me, there was a hidden smile, too. Before he had a chance to say anything, I spoke. "My blood brother, Dull Horn," I said, pointing to the necklace and the cut on the pad of my hand, "has become much sick from his wounds. I have brought him to his clan so he might be healed. He is in danger of dying if we don't hurry."

Almost before I had finished talking, several men were carrying him into the maze of tepees. The great chief motioned for me to follow him. Almost on cue, the rest of the tribe seemed to go about their business. It was as if nothing had happened. Picking up my weapons and Dull Horn's headdress, I followed the chief. After forty paces, he pointed toward his tepee and motioned for me to go in. I bent down and went inside. Bear Claw signaled for me to sit and summoned his squaw for food.

All he said was, "Eat first."

I was served boiled buffalo tongue. I drank the broth and ate the meat with relish. It was well cooked and broke apart in my mouth. "I must check on my brother," I said.

"Later," was Bear Claw's reply. "He being cared for."

"Let me see feet." Bear Claw touched my feet.

I pulled off the traveling moccasins and showed him. They were still cut up but were looking better. He called out and his woman came in and bathed and dressed them. I'm not sure it did any good, but it felt nice to have someone looking after me. I laced my moccasins on over the dressing and looked at him.

"You are brave man," he said. "You have made my clan proud. Rest now! When the sun sets, we look upon your blood brother. You are a Crow! You run the arrow bravely."

He handed me a blanket and motioned for me to lie near the fire. He didn't have to ask me twice. My weapons were where I'd left them as the warrior left me in his tepee. I felt my body melt into the soft reed mat covered with buffalo hide. I was asleep as soon as I lay down. I must have slept about four or five hours. The sun was setting in the sky when I awoke. I could smell meat cooking in the air and the bustle of people getting ready for night. Children were laughing and sticks were being snapped for the evening fire. I sat up and rubbed my eyes and looked about the tepee.

The door opened up and Mighty Bear Claw signaled for me to follow. Folks looked up from their work, but no one seemed to pay much heed to me or mind that I was in camp. The last time I was here, they couldn't wait to get their hands on me . . . or to bury a handy knife or sharp stick in my flesh. Tribes were funny this way and I knew you couldn't think of their behavior in white man's terms.

We entered a smoky tepee, a large one that must have been nearly twenty feet across. Dull Horn was propped up on a willow pallet near the fire, buck naked. A woman was looking after the wounds on his leg while a medicine man was dancing about singing some chant. He looked bad, but at least he was asleep. The medicine man sang a little louder and stopped and shook a little pollen from his bag to the four winds.

He continued doing this until he had done it nearly ten times in a half hour. He called to the Great Spirit. We just sat there and watched. About every fifteen minutes, the medicine woman changed the dressing on his leg. At one point, Dull Horn awoke. His lips trembled and his eyes looked dull and listless. He didn't seem to be so feverish, but he looked awful. I was rather dizzy and light headed from all the smoke. The medicine man had stopped his pollen dance and lit a chunk of sweet grass. It had a sickly smell. I supposed it had a medicine quality, but you couldn't prove it by me. I sorely wanted to stick my head out and get a few breaths of air.

Dull Horn looked at me and smiled weakly. "My blood brother,

Fast Deer Feet," he said. "We are one blood now! I'm your blood and you mine."

He looked up at the chief. "He fight Scar, but not take his hair. He is brave as the great bear. He found and helped me. I have made him one of us. He has the heart of a brave and the wisdom of the wind."

"Yes," said Bear Claw. "He is brave man. We knew he kill not Scar. Scar was brought one sun ago. He has broken leg and torn up body. He has talked little about how."

"You sleep now," Bear Claw said. We went to his tepee. A piece of meat and a few tubers were on a slab of wood when I came in. Someone had built up the fire. After eating, there wasn't much else to do but sleep. I stretched out and shut my eyes.

When I awoke in the morning, the sun was out and the camp was moving. I walked down to the stream and washed my face. The cool water refreshed me. After a light breakfast, I was summoned to a meeting of the braves. Bear Claw asked me to recount what had happened from the time of the run. In my best Crow and with help from one of the braves and Bear Claw, I recounted what had happened. I expanded the fight with Scar and the grizzly bear maybe more than the truth would rightly allow.

I stretched out the fight with the bear and how I ate a chunk of raw heart to gain the heart of the beast. I told about how I had to face Scar man-to-man to make him account for the poor way he'd treated me. I noticed the braves were nodding their heads, following every word. Indians love a good story and are good listeners. They excel at the art of story telling. I drug out how I could have killed Scar, but I let him live so he could think of how he got beat every day of his life. It's harder to live with shame than die with it, I suggested.

The braves smiled. I got the impression that they liked to hear about someone besting Scar, since he was about as popular as a pole cat at high tea. I barely touched upon my fight with Dull Horn . . . other than to say he was a great warrior. I did lie a little to protect him. My story spent more time telling them how we became brothers and how we traveled toward the Crow camp. I talked about how he turned sick after I thought he was on the mend, so I hurried in fast to get him to his healing people.

I mentioned nothing about my furs and truck. It didn't seem like the time to say anything.

"I am pleased to be Fast Deer Feet," I said in a loud voice pounding my chest. "I run like the deer. In my own language my name is Wolf. However, never will I wear a name more proudly than the one given me by my blood brother, Dull Horn."

Touching my necklace and looking wistful, I said, "In a few minutes, I'd like to go and look into the tepee where my brother lies. I hope your Great Spirit will strengthen him."

I quietly walked back to my place and sat down.

Bear Claw stood and started his speech making in fine form. He talked so fast I could barely follow what he was saying. Then I got altogether lost. You had to say your Crow pretty slow, then it needed to be simple, if you wanted me to follow what was being said. I just tried to look stern and happy at the same time, nodding when the other braves nodded. I had a hard time following what was being said. He may have been talking about me, it's hard to say. After all the speechifying, the group broke up. Several braves came and looked at me directly and grunted something of approval.

I wasn't worried about them drilling an arrow or a knife between my shoulder blades. I followed to where Dull Horn was resting and went inside. He looked a little better, but he still looked weathered and weak. The chanting medicine man was gone, but the healing woman was there tending him. She addressed Bear Claw in a fast, excited voice, almost shrill like a song bird.

"She says that Dull Horn is getting better and it is her opinion that he will not fade. He will live. Most of the poison from the wound is gone and he resting. The Great Spirit of our clan is not ready to take him."

Sitting there, it didn't take much to see the wound was looking better. It wasn't as red nor as puffed up. The infection was down and he was healing. Rest and food had done him some good. All the traveling we'd done had set him back. Whatever the medicine woman was putting on his wound and having him drink was helping. I can say the chanting man didn't do as much good as the healing woman—except make it hard to breathe. I kept my thinking to myself since these folks set a lot of store by such things. And you never know how all this healing works. The Mormons set store by prayer healing.

I was glad to see him on the mend. He woke a few times and smiled at me, drank a little something she put up to his lips, then went back to sleep.

I visited him most of the day. He was starting to get his strength back. Several times in the afternoon, he'd talk for a spell. I was pleased to see some sparkle in his eyes. I think the medicine woman was pleased, too, since she'd not slept since he'd been brought to her care. The medicine man only checked in on him several times a day, sometimes dancing about, other times working with pollen.

On the morning of the third day, I got up to check on my friend and saw that all my truck, including my guns, knife, and furs were stacked by the front of the tepee. Across the top was my saddle. I slipped my knife into my belt, but didn't think it would be a good idea to look things over in much detail at this point. It was a sign that they trusted me and viewed me as one of their own. At least I wouldn't have to steal them, which would have been a slight breach of etiquette. It pleased me that they thought enough of me to give me my truck back. I liked these folks.

On my way out, Bear Claw walked by me. "Fast Deer Feet is Crow now. Your horses and four more will be ready when you are."

Before I could say anything, he was gone.

To make the day better, Dull Horn was walking slowly outside when I got to his teepee. We clasped arms and he pointed to the creek. Walking slow, I watched him take a cool drink and bathe his face and arms in the clear water.

I stayed close by for another five days. Each noon, Dull Horn and I would take a progressively longer walk into the nearby forest or plains. I was interested in what plants a man might eat. Dull Horn was a medicine man, so he showed me a number of plants and herbs that could be used for healing or eating. He told me of the sights he'd seen. He was a wanderer, never being satisfied if he was staying at home too long. One time he'd been gone for almost a year. It was not unusual for him to take off for several months at a spell since he loved to see what was over the next hill. He had wandered to the north through the dangerous Black Foot country, then into the land of the Cree where the earth became wet like a swamp. He'd befriended an old Black Foot Medicine man who had gone north past the prairies to the great forests and rivers.

He knew of the Great Basin land across the mountains where the lake had the water of salt. He'd also spent some time in the fire country to the north where the land was angry—the land of the yellow stones.

We talked of wandering north through the fire country.

"I have to get my furs to Mormons by the salt water," I said slowly. "I have given my word to them that I will bring my trappings. But when I am done, I will return to my Crow brother and we will search out the Yellowstone land where the earth is angry or perhaps we will travel to the great forests of the north.

"Or maybe I shall help my new tribe hunt buffalo against the coming of winter."

"That will be good," Dull Horn said with a long grin. "The wind is free to travel where she will. The wind is no better than men. It is good for warriors to see the lands the Great Spirit has made for Mother Earth . . . the land and man are one."

Dull Horn was talking slow so I could catch every word and I have to say I wasn't paying much attention to anything but his story and how blue the sky was and how white the clouds were in the heavens. My fingers were hooked in my belt. I looked down at a tepee and, to my surprise, I gazed into the cold-blooded eyes of Scar. I've looked at friendlier rattlesnakes.

He was on a buffalo robe, leaning against the side of his tepee. His face was drawn and puffy from the fall I'd invited him to take. There was a large splint on his leg and one of his arms was in a sling. Faster than a woman's mood, there was something in his hand as his elbow cocked back and his wrist flicked forward.

All my daydreaming nearly cost me. I wasn't on guard and failed to react swiftly enough. There was shout from Dull Horn as I was brutally knocked off my feet by his flying body. He'd thrown himself at me to keep me from harm's way. Where I'd been standing, a knife was buried into the lodge pole about chest level.

Scar would have killed me in the end if Dull Horn had not shoved me out of the way.

Scar screamed something at me as I got up. Some sort of a white eyes insult. I'd pulled my knife and was upon him. I reached for his good arm and jerked him over so he was on his back. He screamed out as I wrenched his leg into the ground, hopefully re-breaking it.

Kneeing him in the back, I reached for his hair and jerked it back savagely. My intent was to cut that hair he was so proud of, but I got a little too close. He fought my giving him a trimming and I cut down into the top of his skin. I yanked and found that in my anger, I'd accidentally scalped him, ruining forever his vanity over his front hair. Pays to have a sharp knife.

I had to teach him a lesson. Next, I cut off his hair so it was only an inch or so, a great insult among his own. He looked rather silly since I'm not much of a barber.

Scar had broken the hospitality of the tribe which was a serious offense. Without further comment, Bear Claw put him upon a horse backwards, handing him a knife and bow. He told Scar that he was a renegade and that, if he was ever seen by a member of the clan, he would be killed on sight. "You have dishonored our people," he said. "You have broken the laws of the people and must not live among them! Go! Never let the sun fall on your shoulders among the people."

He slapped the horse. Scar's cold expression never changed. I watched him until he was just a speck in the east. I knew he was blaming this on me.

The next morning I planned to leave. I loaded up my horses and noticed that I had more furs than I'd started with. Bear Claw was checking the packs on several of the horses he'd made a present of. "Fur keep your people warm in a cold wind. Will not have Fast Deer Feet's people, brother of the Crow, tremble in the deep snow or shiver in the long night."

Bowing my head, I clasped arms with several braves who were standing by the horses. Mighty Bear Claw, Dull Horn, and several braves would ride with me until we got to the edge of their territory.

We rode the morning out in silence, the wind in our faces, soaking in the sun and looking at the birds of prey sweep across the grassy plain in search of food. We rode steady and fast without rest, the horses eager to cover the trail. We were warriors who had met and fought and learned something about getting along together in a world of hostility and enmity. There was an unwritten bond as old as men, a bond of warriors whose faithfulness was never questioned and whose courage had already been proven.

Never have I ridden with men I was more pleased to call my friends.

I rode sadly since, unlike my Crow friends, I knew their way of life was fated and as fragile as dust in a strong wind. Soon my people would come and I shuddered to think about what would happen. We talk about equality among men, but some states, much to my embarrassment, still held black slaves. And what we'd done with the other tribes we'd *made peace with* in the past didn't give me much comfort. We'd lied and misled. We've given, then taken their land. I wasn't always proud to be an American. We could learn a few things from the good book. We had a lot to learn about being fair and getting on with the red men.

You can say all you want about the Mormons, but they treat Indians with more respect than most. Brigham's motto is that it's easier to be friends and feed 'em than to fight 'em.

We camped that night and feasted on an antelope I shot.

Several of the braves told stories. One told how the Crows first came to have horses and how the Great Spirit had smiled since the horse had allowed men to feed their women and children. Curling up in our blankets by the dying fire, I watched the stars glide across the sky. I didn't feel like sleeping. I felt at home and knew I'd be back.

After a few hours ride, we parted at midmorning. I presented Dull Horn with my knife. It was a keen blade and he smiled. No knife in the tribe had half its quality. I made presents to each of the other braves, my cups and pan—such truck they value highly. I gave Mighty Bear Claw my .52 pistol along with some powder and a handful of shot. I could get another pistol in Salt Lake. I could get another knife, too. Not as good, but something better than a trade knife.

We clasped arms and I turned to go. I told Dull Horn to look for me in the heat of the summer. I didn't look back until I'd ridden several miles and was on a rise. Turning, I waved since they were still bunched up in the place where we'd parted. I'm not sure, but I like to think they waved back.

Below me was the Green. In a couple of days I'd be in Bridger. With the spring wind at my back and the sun in my face, I set a fast pace. I had to get my furs, and any more I might be able to buy in Bridger, to the Salt Lake Basin.

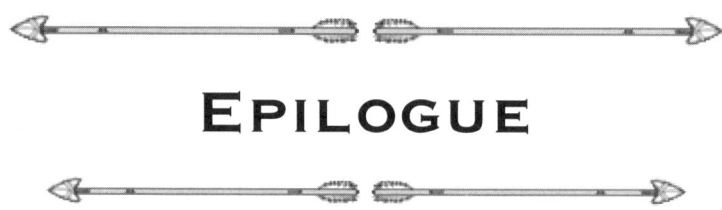

Epilogue

Brigham Young asked me to call on him directly when I came in.

I left word with a storekeeper for cousin Orin Porter. I told him I was back and I'd like to see him before I took off again. I did stop, however, and had myself a good bath and bought some new clothes first. Didn't think it would be polite to sit in a man's home in the same clothes I've lived in for half a year.

Brother Brigham loved to pump you for all the information he could. Not much got past him. Besides, he set a great table and fed you until you were about ready to burst. Duded up for a Sunday meeting, I called on him. I hadn't had fried chicken and all the trimmings in so long I'd forgotten what a good feast tasted like. A couple of his wives brought in a few pies that I made short work of after I had all the chicken I could stuff in.

I managed to bring fifteen horses packed with furs. As always,

Brigham gave me a good price for my skins. Some of the money went to some of the trappers at Bridger who'd be by to take it out in trade at the Mormon's store. The money I got from the furs the Crows gave me I planned to use on supplies for the tribe.

"Brother Wolf," Brigham Young said, "I want to thank you for those furs. They look first-rate and the Saints will use them gladly. As you've guessed, we have our eye on the Cache country, but it will be a few more years before we're ready to settle there.

"By the way, it sounds like you made friends with that tribe of Crow Indians. You did a fine piece of work. Did you tell them about the Book of Mormon?"

He had a way of making me feel comfortable, even though I'm just a country boy. "Well sir," I said. "I'm not a member of your church."

Brigham smiled. "All in good time, Wolf. All in good time. You'll know when you're ready. Nevertheless, you've helped the Saints. Since you're going back, I'd like you to take some presents in the name of the church."

I really didn't know what to say. I looked into eyes that seemed to look through me. It made you want to quit swearing and such, but it wasn't enough to make me join up and give up the mountain ways.

"Wolf," he said. "I'd like to enlist your help. You were talking about going back and heading into the Yellowstone country or maybe going north."

"Yes sir," I said.

"What would you think of traveling north and taking a good hard look. A long way north. One day the Saints will be moving into Canada and I have a mission for you. There's a Catholic priest, a Father DeSmet, working with the Crees. I'd like you to look for him.

"The church will pay for your supplies and I'll pay you a sum now and when you return. When do you think you could go?"

"I could be ready the day after tomorrow, sir," I said.

"Good! Come back tomorrow and I'll explain what I want you to find in detail. In a dream I saw the Lord's saints in Canada."